Karolinum Press

MODERN CZECH CLASSICS

# Libuše Moníková
# Transfigured Night

Translated from the German by Anne Posten
Afterword by Helga G. Braunbeck

KAROLINUM PRESS 2023

KAROLINUM PRESS
Karolinum Press is a publishing department
of Charles University
Ovocný trh 560/5, 116 36 Prague 1
Czech Republic
www.karolinum.cz

Cataloguing-in-Publication Data is available
from the National Library of the Czech Republic

ISBN: 978-80-246-5172-9
ISBN: 978-80-246-5302-0 (pdf)
ISBN: 978-80-246-5304-4 (mobi)
ISBN: 978-80-246-5303-7 (epub)

# CONTENTS

Chapter 1    /7
Chapter 2    /24
Chapter 3    /38
Chapter 4    /52
Chapter 5    /59
Chapter 6    /65
Chapter 7    /94

Afterword    /107
Translator's Note    /122
About the Translator    /126

# 1.

Malovanka, Marijánka, Drinopol: the third stop from Po-hořelec, formerly known as the "Memorial of National Literature"; the names have been changing in quick succession for a while now. Strahov Monastery was given back to the Premonstratensians as part of the restitution; who knows how long the National Literature will stay there. The old name Pohořelec—scene of the fire—has remained, a reminder of the frequent blazes here in the suburb of Hradčany. I get off. The 22 tram continues on, past the "Chestnut Tree" inn where the Social Democratic Party was founded, on to the Street of the Pioneers, home to the oldest male monastery in Bohemia and St. Margaret's church, toward Bílá Hora, "White Mountain," where the army of the Bohemian Protestant nobility was destroyed in battle in 1620. Last stop.

After November 1989 the Street of the Pioneers was renamed Patočka Street in memory of the philosopher Jan Patočka, co-founder of Charta 77, who died at seventy of a stroke after eleven hours of questioning by the StB, the secret police. A police helicopter rattled above his funeral in the cemetery of St. Margaret's, drowning out the speakers. Anyone who approached the cemetery was filmed, anyone who wanted to enter had to show identification and was put on a list.

I get out at Drinopol, maybe from *drnopal*: "wood burner," "coal-maker"—there might have been a charcoal pile here once. I never used to think about names at all, they were taken for granted, if not always clear; back then this unclarity was familiar. Now I'm not sure of a single word. I cross the street, past the inn on the corner, and up the steep steps to Strahov Hill. Here the streets continue upward at a more leisurely pace. The building I'm looking for is on my downhill side, I can already see it. Never lose altitude: old mountain climbing wisdom.

I haven't been in this area for a long time. I continue along the ridge. The streets turn into paths: narrow, convoluted, ending in orchards and shrubbery where refuse has collected. Plastic, discarded bottles. There's hoarfrost on the rusty green grass. An icy staircase, the railing broken. I pull myself up using grass and brush, avoiding branches and thorns. The familiarity of old shortcuts and cut-throughs—overgrown trails, crumbling stairs, blocked paths, no winter maintenance: enter at your own risk. Who else's?

I reach the stadium.

There's also another way, when coming from the city. Via Petřín, the *Laurenziberg* in German. This could have been the site of Josef K.'s abandoned quarry; now the ground has been leveled—a vast plain, with one of the largest stadiums in the world, surrounded by three smaller ones and other athletic facilities. The stadium stands on the far side of Petřín, facing westwards, away from the city, not visible from the Charles Bridge; from there you can only see the observation tower. This panorama path behind the observation tower, with the Vltava in the valley and the slopes and orchards of the Malá Strana at one's feet, is pretty.

The third way, the shortest, leads behind the Memorial of National Literature, running parallel to the Hunger Wall, directly to the stadium: a wide street, *Spartakiádní*, with the defunct Dlabačov station, where special tram lines and rerouted trams brought gymnasts to the republic's greatest sports festival every five years for weeks on end.

The tracks, the platform islands still exist, the stairs that lead, via iron bridges, to the Street of the Spartakiad. No more trams run along turning loops. Sometimes a defective tram car is parked here and then disappears; no one embarks.

The stadium is abandoned, as are the paths between the various facilities: Street of the Walkers, the Runners, the Discus Throwers, the Fencers, the Riders, Street of the Athletes, the Motorcyclists; the simplicity of the names suits the size the of the complex. The gates, closed off with barbed wire and security fencing, still feel gigantic. The bleachers, which I reach after climbing over multiple barriers, are decrepit, the benches and steps broken, the concrete brutally bare of plaster, as if the building is meant to keep the masses in check—Piranesi's *Carceri*, not designed for humans, airier but similarly dismal under the overhangs.

I hear cries from a thousand throats; soldiers streaming in through the portals at a gallop, their bare upper bodies sweaty with heat and exertion, their skin gleaming in the sun.

Strahov Stadium, where I twice tumbled as a schoolgirl at the "National Spartakiad"—that mass gymnastics festival so beloved by the Communists. The first time with a cube: red for girls, yellow for boys. Since we weren't evenly split in my class, I was a boy for gymnastics purposes, with a yellow cube, red gym shorts, and a white tank top. Strahov Stadium could hold 16,000 gymnasts and 220,000 spectators, which regularly made the Soviet delegations—I never saw a Russian walk through the city alone—pale with envy. The performances were sold-out throughout the Spartakiad.

My mother sewed and pasted together my first cube out of gray cardboard. It became so weak and dented from all the holding and tossing that several times it caused the cubes stacked on top of it in a pyramid to come tumbling down. Then I finally got a proper cube for the performance—in the wrong color.

The highpoint of the gymnastics show was always a stunt in which the whole group created a design, the tumbling bodies at rest, the gymnastics equipment pushed together—then the next movement, from inside to out, from left to right, and the mosaic would unfold into a new design for the spectators in the stands, a kaleidoscope of insipidity accompanied by swelling music from the loudspeakers and versification. About the beauty of our country, about peace, the threat of war from the West, and how we had to be ever on guard. Then running back to the white place markers, pivoting, and doing the next figure, cubes raised.

The second time, five years later, as a *dorostenka*, an "adolescent," with a white plastic hoop: similar movements, similar patterns, just less angular; we were fifteen. Outside of practice we used the hoops to experiment with hula hooping.

As we marched through the gates, Slovaks and Moravians among us—for many of them it was their first visit to the capital; the next group already streaming out of the barracks in the heat, gathering for their performances, the children wound up: crying fits, diarrhea, sunstroke, thirst—I read the motto over the portal: Socialism has triumphed here! From then on we weren't just the ČSR, the Czechoslovak Republic, but the ČSSR; it was 1960.

Every level of society and all ages participated in the Spartakiad: pre-school children hopping around a maypole with their leaders, or those in the alternative program with their parents, illustrating their carefree daily lives, and pensioners who didn't want to be left behind, former head gymnasts.

The gymnastics of the women: forty- and fifty-year-old workers and employees who met regularly after work to practice their routines, pressured and spurred on by the factory's squad leaders, but also taking perceptible pleasure in the change of pace, in moving their bodies, away from their families and housework. Their program was even simpler than the hoop routines; their props were colorful cloths, stuck into their elastic belts. The more advanced among them swung clubs, but the movements were the same.

For a year we practiced once a week, at first without music, then intensively in the last six months. Regular gym class in school was cancelled: no ball sports, no pommel horse, no races. We stood on the place markers and waited for our entrance; then run two meters to the left, turn, two meters to the right, turn, pivot to the left, pivot to the right, lift and lower the hoop, roll it over the back of the hand, run to the left, to the right, back to the marker, turn. The real task was finding the right marker again at the end.

Only when watching other groups—we were given a few tickets to the morning shows as a reward—did it become clear how many slip-ups there were, how many strays who couldn't find their markers; the others went on with the routine, the lost ones ran to and fro, trying to push others off their markers, sometimes it was *their* marker. And the deputy secretaries in the stands, heavy from long sitting, watched this frenzy in ecstatics, clapping with enthusiasm and emotion.

Choreographers, composers, and poets earned well from the state commissions, likewise the industry that provided the uniforms: leotards, tricotine skirts—red, with dashed white flowers, elastic at the waist, the same size for all adults; special sizes were snapped up immediately. The skirts were worn even in the city; the closer to Strahov, the more scantily-clad the women.

The people in gym shorts could be seen on the streets: *dorostenky* in short jerseys, who thrilled the soldiers looking out the barracks windows of Hradčany; but old women too, workers with varicose veins, their bellies spilling out over too-taut belts, flabby thighs and upper arms, sweaty armpits, laughing, walking through the streets in collective euphoria as if it were the most natural thing in the world. In their Moravian slang, they called out to each other:

*"baby!"* and *"děcka!"*—"chicks!" "kiddos!" After the district and regional Spartakiads, Strahov was the highpoint, their homeland was a vast place.

The shamelessness was contagious. Women, who performed trivial movements and hops in the stadium, united in their anxiety not to make a mistake, laughed giddily when they were teased by the men outside.

The Spartakiad was a celebration of exhibitionism, awakening the used-up, lifeless bodies.

What was striking in both sexes: the varicose veins, the statewide predisposition to weak connective tissue, the various levels of wear and tear.

The women, broken by work—by family, children, and men. The men, broken by beer.

The young people looked different.

As an alternative to routines with hoops, there was a mixed program with girls and boys together, with gymnastic interludes, technically more challenging. All participants had to be able to do at least simple flips and be in good shape, the tempo was faster.

*"Zapalte ohně na horách, zapalte ohně v lidských srdcích!"*—"Light fires in the mountains, light fires in human hearts!" An emphatic female voice recited the introductory verses, the tribute to *our* Slovaks and their national uprising, with allusion to the traditional fires in the Tatras, cherished as shared folklore—then drums, and the gymnasts swarmed out, spread across the whole field. Riotous applause: even the entrance was thrilling. At the end, near evening, they lit their torches, more impressive than our hoops.

But the soldiers were the highpoint. In white gym shorts, tanned for their performance. The closed circles of bodies turned in opposite directions: the inner circle to the right, the outer to the left, their limbs wove into the base of a pyramid, the next ones climbed onto their shoulders, forming a second level, then another circle, a third level. And at the top stood someone who jumped; he climbed up the bare shoulders of the others and jumped, and his comrades below formed a corridor and caught him. Over the years several people died during training and plenty more were hurt: badly caught, the white shorts transformed into mud-smeared tatters over the course of the performance; the program was only interrupted in the case of heavy rain.

Pictures kept secret for thirty years show faces contorted with effort and pain, feet crushing the fingers of those beneath them, slipping into faces and pulling hair, smushed noses, gashed eyebrows, bloody foreheads. The hundreds of thousands in the stands stood in their places and shouted in rapture.

At the first Spartakiad in 1955, the bleachers were lined with emblems made of papier-maché, the crests of the people's democracies: the Polish flag drawn as a coat of arms, next to the Romanian, Hungarian, Bulgarian, East German, Chinese. The huge letters, legible from far away: *CCCP*. Next to every crest waved the Czechoslovakian and Soviet flags, in close communion.

Folklore ensembles danced on the lawn as a prelude: women with three or four skirts layered over each other, and embroidered bodices, starched blouses, boots, bows in their hair. Accompanied by cimbalom and violin music. Folklore—that was something from Slovakia and Moravia; Bohemian folklore had never been very fiery.

Recordings from the fifties, recently shown on television, provoked a wave of emotion and enthusiasm, so that the program directors considered running them a second time, accompanied by explanatory, off-putting commentary.

The living images of the Spartakiad. One could have made different images than bouquets and pyramids out of the thousands of bodies all devoted to the shared cause: flags, maps, mottos, crests. The biggest: the head of Stalin, with a pipe that smokes or stops depending on the movements of the people; smiling, serious, wrinkled brow—the face transforms like cigarette ads on mobile projection surfaces. With eyes that look directly at each of the 220,000 spectators.

My youth.

I go back to the steep street above Drinopol. The building isn't locked as most are now, even in this part of town. The high number of the "amnestied" who are blamed for the broken phonebooths and vending machines, the Roma from Slovakia who feel at home in Prague, the gangs of "Mützler" from Russia and Ukraine who get into bloody fights with each other, as well as the burdensome and constantly increasing masses of tourists, make the people of the city edgy and suspicious.

The door scrapes as I open it and scratches a light quarter circle in the dark tiled floor. Noises from behind the left-hand door, but no nosy old woman appears to ask who I'm looking for. The name board in the stairwell is yellowed and some names are missing, but the empty slots are by no means a suggestion that there are apartments free here. The name I'm looking for is on the top floor. I climb the stairs, my right knee is stiff—I strained a tendon last rehearsal. The fellow student I'm visiting was exempt from gymnastics. I want to surprise him—a whim, as if I've reverted to my schooldays, to the Prague 6 neighborhood of my childhood.

*RNDr. Radomil Nechvátal.* I ring. I wait. I ring again. Shuffling steps behind the door. Who's there?

I say my name. Silence. Who? I repeat it.

He opens the door hesitantly, stares at me. He stands there in baggy sweatpants that flop around his legs, a shapeless waist: this is not a sporty person. I should have called first.

He says *Ahoj* and waits to see if I'll offer him my hand. I take a step back—this is worse than I imagined.

He says, Should I change? I wasn't expecting anyone.

I say, Put something on.

Yes, can you wait? Outside, in the hallway.

I say I'll wait in the room or in the kitchen. I don't know how many rooms he has; in Prague most bachelors just have one, a room plus kitchen and bathroom. Even that much is luxury.

The narrow hallway is made narrower by a row of cabinets, full of dusty glasses where, upon closer inspection, I see something move. The stink is so strong that I want to turn around on the spot, but he's already closed the apartment door. He wedges his way past me and leads me into a room with more shelves, this time filled mostly with books, but also with two terraria, a wardrobe, and in the middle, an unmade bed. The room is gloomy, with a slanted wall. I go to open the window first thing, but it can only be cracked. I try to look out, but above me there's only the gray, overcast sky, which is now rapidly darkening. He comes back, still buttoning the pants he's put on. "Betelgeuze," he points upward. "In the south. Right above my head at night. The red giant. Alpha in Orion."

He knows he can get me with words and facts. "First magnitude. The diameter more than three times as big as the distance between the sun and the earth."

He stands close behind me, I can hardly move. "You can't see any stars now!" I say petulantly and walk out. He closes the window behind me. We go into the kitchen, which is also the living room and study. I ask for an ashtray. After a laborious, reluctant search, he brings me a saucer. I know that he's confused, clumsy and ridiculous, and I'm brusque, as if to punish him for my coming by after twenty years.

Out of embarrassment he tries the familiar school tone, *boy pupil teases girl pupil*, though in his case it was more the opposite. An only child of older parents, delivered by forceps, which dented his head and left him physically handicapped but with a kind of super-brain. Science, philosophy, even literature to some degree. He would write, bring his stuff to me to read; I would criticize it smugly, as one does at sixteen—science fiction didn't interest me. The stories were good.

Now he shows me an anthology: international authors, Lem, Asimov, and a story by him. "If you'll bring it back, I can lend it to you," he says.

This embarrassing situation is my own fault. I make a face, but this air kills any desire for sarcasm. "Can you open the window?" I ask. I'm genuinely feeling nauseous now.

He wraps himself conspicuously in a horrible cardigan, shuffles to the window. "Do you want to see microbats?" He leans out.

I fall for it. "Where?"

"There, beyond the roof beam."

"I don't see any."

"Not yet, but in half an hour. They're nocturnal."

"I know that!" I'm getting angry. "And what's in the cabinets?"

"Wax moths." He points to a honeycomb in a glass with moths on it, they're in the chambers and on the bottom of the glass as well: filthy, fungous, pupal. The heavy, sweetish smell is hard to bear. "Chloroform," he says, "$CHCl_3$, trichloromethane."

I want to leave. Instead I ask: "Why chloroform?"

"Don't worry," he laughs, "I'm not addicted. Was it Trakl?"

I don't know what disgusts me more: that he's so pathetic or that he's so conceited.

"It sterilizes the honeycombs," he says. "Against mites, and whatever the moths bring with them. The moth larvae eat wax and destroy hives. *Galleria mellonella*, also called beewolf. Although that's also a name for hornets," he smiles. "I mean the moths. We're trying to fight them. I put antibiotics in their food, knead penicillin into the wax. The larvae, you see, these little grubs, get infected with fungi and die."

"Isn't it rather expensive?" I ask.

"Unpurified penicillin is cheap. It doesn't need complicated galenics. I worked in the purification department. Potassium acetate, precisely calibrated to pH 7.8. Anyway, it's not for mass application, just for basic research."

I think about the word galenics.

"They become infected to different degrees," he continues. "When the infection is mild, the larvae manage to pupate and hatch. Then the imagoes are infected with fungus, the adults."

I bend over the glasses. The moths careen, in varying stages of agony, full of dirt and dust they crawl, distempered, dead bees between them on the bottom of the glass, stuck clumps of wax, filth.

"And the bees?"

"They're immune. They produce antibiotics themselves, in the honey. If you eat honey, you don't need penicillin."

"I don't take penicillin," I say.

A disgusting warmth rises off the glasses. He doesn't seem to notice it, nor the stink either. This warmth is his room temperature. He doesn't want it any colder. "Another option would be to inoculate them with an overdose of juvenile hormone," he says. "It can be extracted. Then they wouldn't pupate."

"Each larva individually?"

"Yes, but it's expensive. More expensive than iridium."

"This is your idea of basic research." I stand looking at an empty aquarium. It's almost a welcome sight.

"I'm going to put fish in it," he says. "I want cichlids. They're the most intelligent." He talks of *Aequidens*, *Geophagus*, *Cichlasoma*, and *Astronotus*.

"Yes, they're the most intelligent," I say, "but your tank is too small. Stick with oscars or dwarf angels."

We got along once, I kept aquariums too, but now that I don't have a permanent home and just rove around, I can't keep any animals, any plants. Nor do I have pictures on the walls—posters sometimes, which change frequently. He asks where I stay when I'm in Prague.

"Close by. Below Drinopol, if you take the steps down from the tram. But I'm not often here."

"I usually take the bus," he says. "It stops here on the corner. I don't go down to the tram, and I certainly don't take the stairs back up. But I'll keep it in mind."

I'm dizzy from the air, tired and strangely passive. I sit down on an uncomfortable chair, on a dirty rag, a kind of pad. He sits and watches me.

I always used to have the impression that he'd developed a particular kind of vigilance in regard to me, as if he were always on the lookout, waiting for a moment when I wasn't paying attention. He would call periodically, wanting to meet. Ninety-nine percent of the time I would have laughed at him, but almost always he managed to catch me at the one percent, when I was distracted or in an unusually good mood, so that I found the notion amusing and went. During our walks I couldn't look at him, I found him physically repulsive, and that too had a certain allure. The contrast between us couldn't have been greater: I danced tap and ballet and he could hardly move. But he was the most interesting person in school.

Once he said to me: I wish you were in a wheelchair so that you couldn't run away, and I'd push you wherever I felt like.

We kept up these odd meetings after graduation, twice, three times a year, actually it was the only relationship I kept up with anyone from our class. Usually we went to the theatre; he knew that took the least convincing. We went to plays that were sold out; he'd stood in line for hours to get the tickets.

Once he actually dared to ask me if I would marry him. After the performance I was in a particularly relaxed frame of mind and just laughed, asked him how he pictured it. And he told me. His fantasy was so clear that it sent shivers down my spine. The wheelchair came into it at some point.

He placed personal ads and went on the dates that resulted. I asked him about it and he told me reluctantly. From his reports I came to understand that there were a lot of women who seemed to be afraid of ending up alone, and that he had a real chance. It wasn't only handicapped women, in fact hardly any: many had studied, but the men—legless, toothless, blind, deaf, poor, drunkards, ill, without exception poorly educated—had their pick. The system saw to it that even the most underprivileged man saw himself as somebody when he had a woman on his arm.

He kept up the correspondence under pressure from his mother, who was afraid he wouldn't be provided for after her death. He took a pompous tone when he talked about the women; he usually let them wait for him.

I always let him wait for me: half an hour, three quarters, sometimes even a whole hour. Then I'd call his house, I knew he'd call his mother to say he'd be late. I'd have her tell him I wasn't coming. Then his mother had me on the line. "Fräulein Lena, I can call you that can't I, or Loonora, it's lovely of you to call, and that you go out with our Radek now and then, you know he so admires you. It's a shame that you can't manage it today, but maybe next time?"

Mothers of unmarried sons loved me. I could bewitch them. The sons were unimportant, but a mother—mine had died too early. It was the mothers I wanted to get to, not the sons.

How's your mother, I ask. He sits across from me: bloated, mostly gray already, glasses—the same kind he's had for thirty years, black rectangular frames, only the lenses have gotten thicker. The boil on his chin has become a discolored bulge, actually it's hardly any worse than it used to be; at fifteen, sixteen, parents would greet him respectfully in the halls at school, thinking he was a teacher. He'd always looked old.

He had a high, squeaky voice and phlegmy speech; speaking, moving his facial muscles, was hard for him, that had remained the same.

His father is dead, at the moment his mother is very ill, she always used to come, make him food for the whole week, and clean. You can tell she's not been for a long time. And now he's looking at my boots like I ought to take them off.

I ask about his work. Since getting his doctorate he's worked as a microbiologist in a pharmacological institute near Prague; his newest specialty is biochemistry, but also general chemistry and nuclear chemistry, the latter a private interest. Precipitate, isomerization, ligand field theory: he says the words as if accidentally, knowing they'll have an effect on me. We were the first in our class to get doctorates, he as a biologist, I in literature, Czech studies/German studies: On *The Lament of the "Ackermann aus Böhmen"* by Johannes von Saaz, compared with several motifs in the "Kronika česká" by Václav Hájek von Libočany. He knows that I can become addicted to words.

He asks nothing. Even though he might have seen my picture in the newspaper: well-known "compatriot," artistic director of an international dance company, making a first guest appearance in her hometown on the ten-year anniversary of the ensemble's foundation. She herself, having left the country in 1971, spent ten years teaching literature at various German universities, then founded a dance company which focused on adaptations of modern literature. Her starring role: leading lady in Čapek's/Janáček's *The Makro-*

*pulos Affair*, in her own arrangement. Special circumstance: the similarity of her name to that of the character, perhaps an artistic pseudonym: Leonora Marty.

What the newspapers don't know is that the celebrated compatriot didn't leave with her ensemble, but is staying an extra week in her rented apartment in Prague 6, privately. I want the city to myself.

My former fellow pupil isn't interested; the last time he was in the theatre was with me. Or he doesn't trust himself. He just says: you haven't changed at all. It sounds like a reproach.

I stay longer than I meant to, I had just wanted to surprise him and leave. I had wanted to see his confusion.

He too says that my appearances have something of the quality of an ambush. At first he'd asked if he should make tea. I said later. Then he forgets, or in any case no longer asks. I'd be happy to let him rummage in his cupboards for a clean teacup. Now I don't even smoke.

When I leave, will I shake his hand? Probably not.

I see his face near mine. The light in the hallway is so weak that his features become softer. He brushes me with his shoulder, clumsily, almost inevitably, in the narrow hall. Trying to support himself, he accidentally touches my breast. He breathes heavily, his glasses fog, he takes them off and sets them down blindly on the dusty cabinet.

"What is it that's crawling in there," I ask.

"Newts, *Triturus cristatus*, and alpine salamander . . . *Adelphophagie*, he murmurs.

I don't know what upsets me about the fact that the first fertilized egg, the first embryo, eats all the subsequent ones in the womb. Maybe it's really just the name. It's also that I see his eyes, unprotected without his glasses: big, with long lashes. I see the loneliness in them and a stubborn old desperation. He comes closer. I unbutton my blouse. It's not pity, I'm actually excited. He stares at me, doesn't dare to make a move. I lean forward slightly. He stretches his hand toward me in terror, always prepared for me to laugh him down. I don't move. He touches me with his other hand, more fiercely. Slowly, blindly, he bends to my bosom and touches his mouth to my nipple, sucks hard. I feel his teeth and wince, but now he's got me. He clasps my hips with both his arms, pulls me to the ground with a terrible, unexpected strength. I strain, try to get free, he wheezes and doesn't let go, groans, then he grasps my shoulders and buries his face in my neck, emits slobbering, yelping sobs, trembles. I push him away, pull my coat closed and turn toward the door. "When are you coming back?" he breathes heavily. "Never!" I can't get the door open, something's stuck. He searches laboriously for his glasses, then opens a latch—what can he still be afraid of? He comes outside the door with me. His slowness enrages me, I wish the door would close behind him and he'd have to ring somewhere, get the housemistress, but as reclusive as he is, he won't have left a key with anyone in the building.

He stretches out his hand in the crazy hope of touching me again. I laugh and turn away. He stands in the doorway and calls out after me, it sounds like a curse. I've got him for the next twenty years now for sure. I go down the stairs shuddering, exhilarated, but the exhilaration is short-lived: outside, disgust prevails. I know myself, the feeling of needing to wash my hands quickly before touching something new, before starting anything. My body reacts unerringly to my escapades and encounters. I always get nauseous long before the others realize that someone's an informant, a pig. Or just physically horrid.

I have to wash my hands immediately after touching most people.

That night I have a dream: N. takes two wine glasses out of the cupboard, and a bottle that he couldn't possibly have.

The glasses had been stood upside down and leave dark circles on the dusty shelf.

A bit of filth is stuck on the glass he hands me, a cocoon that hatches a big moth when I turn it. Still wet, sticky, it flutters out, confused. Blinded, it flies into my eye, brushes my cheek, gets caught in my hair, and leaves dust from its wings on my neck. The dusty spot starts to burn, little marks, bloody openings, the skin is raw, red, more and more marks bleed where specks of dust fell from this bred mutant. The biochemist looks on with interest, my immobile schoolmate who wants me in a wheelchair. My shoulder is numb, the paralysis extends through my neck, my shoulder, it remains in my right arm as a constant pain. I wake up.

My neck burns at the spot where I was stung six years ago in the Bay of Biscay by a veiled medusa, a Portuguese man o' war. The paralysis had extended from my shoulder into my arm, I couldn't turn my head or move my arm. I had a hard time reaching the shore, the sea was stormy that day. Swimming was prohibited, but as an inlander I had missed all the warning signs, all the flags. The spot where he'd pressed his wet face.

I stare at the poster on the wall in front of me. A woman leaping across the stage in a high arc, the towers of the city in the background. She takes up the whole poster, her movements transform space and time. A fury in billowing robes with a face that could be three hundred years old or thirty. Emilia or Leonora Marty.

The woman is me.

## 2

It's getting colder. The heat in the apartment doesn't work, I have a little radiator that keeps the temperature in the room just bearable; the hallway and bathroom remain unheated. Outside it's minus twelve degrees. I fall into apathy, want to work, but my notes have disappeared, the pad with the drawings too.

The sketch for *Viktorka* was almost done. Viktorka, pale, confused Viktorka from Božena Němcová's *The Grandmother*. I think about who could dance the role. Jana, Laura?

The story of Viktorka had touched me even as a child. The beautiful farmer's daughter who rejects all the suitors; only the best dancers at the Sunday dances won her favor. Until soldiers came to the village and one of the men from the regiment began to follow her: the "black soldier." She lost all joy in dancing, hardly left the house, became frightened when she was alone, and felt his black eyes everywhere, following her every move. She no longer wanted to stay in the village, and she was quickly engaged to a boy from elsewhere just so that she could get away from the soldier and his uncanny looks. Though some in the village grumbled that a local boy wasn't good enough for her, everything seemed to be looking up. Preparations for the wedding were underway, Viktorka was optimistic. Once she felt brave enough to go out to cut grass alone. She went out with a light heart, carefree, but she was brought back pale, hurt, her wounded foot bound with a fine cloth, and the amulet that the blacksmith's wife had given her to protect her from the evil eye was gone: she had given it to the soldier. He had tended to her out in the field when she'd stepped on a thorn, and confessed his love to her. From then on, Viktorka seemed bewitched. She did not speak, kept delaying the wedding and putting off the groom, and soon not even the parents believed it would actually happen. Finally the regiment left the village, and a few days later Viktorka disappeared as well—following the black soldier. Her father went to look for her but came back empty-handed, and no one had seen her.

Viktorka did not return. A year later a gamekeeper saw a female figure in the woods: unkempt, wild, barefoot, with long black hair, and a swollen belly. Shortly thereafter, on a moonlit night, he saw her go down to the dam and throw a bundle into the water and laugh wildly. It became Viktorka's ritual to sing the dead child a lullaby at the dam every night. During the day she lived in hiding and slept in an overgrown cave. No one could convince her to enter a house, neither the gamekeeper nor her family. When she grew too hungry, she would come to the door, wait, and then leave with a piece of bread. When her father was on his deathbed, she came and allowed herself to be led into the room. She held a cowslip in her hand and played absently with the flower. Her father tried to raise his hand to her, and confusedly she gave him the cowslip. Her mother began to weep. Hearing so many voices, Viktorka looked wildly around her and fled out the door. Years later she was struck by lightning in a storm. They laid her out in the gamekeeper's lodge, her head on a pillow of moss, her hair combed, a wreath of catchflies around her head. Her face had stopped twitching wildly, her restless eyes were closed, but a bitter smile remained on her lips. Thus did the children and the grandmother see her when they went to bid her farewell, the eldest among them Barunka, Božena Němcová.

For this material, I need Janáček. Strange that he'd never adapted the story of Viktorka himself. He'd set "Maryčka Magdónova" and "Kantor Halfar" from Petr Bezruč's *Silesian Songs,* and *The Diary of One Who Disappeared* has a similar theme, though less tragic. Moravian stories, all of them; *The Grandmother* is set in the mountains of Northern Bohemia.

There's music for *Viktorka* already. Fidich? Suk? But I'm thinking of Janáček. There are parts of his *Sinfonietta* that seem made for this—the beginning of the Andante, or the Allegretto, but there are also appropriate passages in *Taras Bulba* and *Jenůfa*. I imagine Jiří Kylián's version with the Netherlands *dans theater*, dedicated to his Moravian grandmother. His *Sinfonietta* is peerless, as is his *L'enfant et les sortilèges*. He had an ensemble, while in my version Viktorka will dance solo, along with the black soldier and the groom. The villagers on the margins, maybe even the grandmother too. —To name a ballet *The Grandmother*. I'll dance the Countess at most: marginal, static. I hear the music in my head and jot down the figures, the movements. Janáček has the same drama, the same tension.

I left the folder in my hotel when I moved out. I could call, but I'd have to find the number and a telephone: this apartment has no service. All of the phone booths in this area are wrecked or just swallow the coins I've saved up without giving me anything in return. A familiar affliction that tempts one to enter any intact phonebooth on sight and start calling people indiscriminately, even when one has nothing to say. For this reason, most of the city's working phonebooths are permanently occupied.

When I have something to take care of in this city, I get tense in advance, irritated and impatient—from the start I'm convinced that it won't work out. I defer errands and delay trips to official agencies, sometimes until the agency itself has shut down. When I want nothing from the city I get along with it best, stumbling across corners and buildings that I know only from books and assumed lost or nonexistent in reality. I give myself over to the surreal feeling of being in this city. There are places that speak to me immediately: Italian cities, New York. In Prague this is accompanied by the feeling of a special distinction. As if I must have done something big or important in a former life to have been born in this city and get to live in it. Though you can hardly breathe the air, and the developments on the horizon are so brutal it seems the city planners must have all been cretins or felons. The modern buildings in East Berlin, or on the outskirts of Salerno or Paris are no better, but in those cities I don't have the same fear.

I start shaking; it occurs to me that I could go swimming to warm myself. I make tea, eat half a yogurt—recently the stores have become filled with Western products, even dairy products, that all taste of thickeners and still are more expensive than the local wares. You have to get up early to get Czech yogurt—and the same goes for the newspaper and a few other necessities. How do the pensioners deal with these soaring prices? You'd think criminality would be on the rise among the 60-year-old set; instead it's the many "entrepreneurs" under thirty, former waiters who had offered their services to the police as thugs, informants, and moneychangers, and now have bought up all the pubs with the profits of their earlier industriousness. In malapropism-riddled English and German they tout their "old Bohemian" cuisine: dumplings from instant packets, "rise salad in vegetarian," the empty tables with dingy old "reserved" slips waiting for tourists with Western currency, like in the old Socialist days. Czech-speaking patrons are hardly allowed in, often only after a hefty bribe, and even then the service is rude and slow. Only émigrés could afford a restaurant meal anyway. In the "kosher" restaurant in the old city, the new owner, a Slovak though he could just as easily be a Czech—names the same prices to a former Resistance fighter and an American tourist, saying that in America he couldn't get a place setting for under twenty dollars. A Klondike mentality proliferates: the arcades in the center, which once housed movie theaters, are now full of imported trash, mass-produced goods from Hong Kong and Taiwan, artificially ripped pants with patches, grommets, and holes, jackets and jerseys with flashy sayings, plus music, cranked all the way up, a different tune coming from each stand. A flood of plastic. The Russian mafia have claimed the best location, where they sell their *Matrjoški*, the pregnant dolls—who've lately begun to bear the faces of politicians—as well as heavy watches and military caps to Western tourists, who don't have a clue and enjoy retrospectively creeping themselves out with the Red Scare.

I gather my swimming stuff. I could walk via the Castle District, down to Klárov, over the bridge, and then take the 17 to the pool in Podolí.

Since I want to inquire at the hotel first, I take the metro. The hotel is above the Nusle Bridge on the C line, it has a good view of the city. They remember me at reception. They'd wanted to stick me in a back room because I spoke Czech; my ensuing tantrum had caused some confusion. I've come back after long years away and want to see the city, I'd said, not some dump behind the hotel with a view of developments that weren't there before and aren't part of the city for me. The unusual word *rumiště* must have made an impression on the porter—it means a kind of distinguished dump. They gave me the king suite. Maybe it had also been my facial expression.

The king suite had two spacious rooms with two baths, but the view was the real prize. Because of the view, I'd invited all the acquaintances and former schoolmates who'd come to our performance; they'd wrinkled their noses: the hotel, a concrete block from the seventies, didn't interest the Praguers, I could only entice them with the promise of a vista. An invitation to view their own city.

The next day I looked out from the other side, from the windows of Prague Castle. The view from the hotel was nicer: you couldn't see the hotel, and above all you couldn't see the television tower. We didn't turn on the lights, the glow from the Castle District was bright enough, like a ship, until midnight. Just women. The darker it grew, the cozier we became. Now and then someone would stand up, go to the bathroom or look out the windows, roam through the rooms, we saw only shadows and heard voices, the groupings changed, we sat on the floor and talked non-stop: there was a lot to catch up on. When the waiter brought coffee we didn't even let him in, he set the tray down outside the door. I miss Czech women.

That's why I remember this hotel with gratitude. The breakfast, too: roasted carp in butter, kept hot under lids in silver chafing dishes. Only one person from our dance company tried it, and the others considered the sweet dishes an affront anyway. They watched in astonishment as I transformed before their eyes: I tucked in greedily, as if I'd been hungry for years.

My notes aren't there, they were found and given to someone else in the group, so now they're long-since out of the country. The head receptionist is solicitous, expresses regret in three languages, including Czech. I see a telephone in the vestibule, make a quick call, the coin gets stuck and doesn't fall into the coin box. A machine that not only doesn't steal, but even gives the money back. I could still call someone, but at the moment I don't know who. I leave. There's a floral display in the middle of the big automatic revolving door; it didn't used to be there. The first thing I noticed in the West: the flower shops. The true Western advantages—flowers and copy machines.

I walk over the bridge, past the new "Palace of Culture," to Vyšehrad. The Palace of Culture is built in the same spirit as the hotel, just somewhat shorter, you can't get as a good a panorama of the city. Originally they had invited us to perform there. If there's anything I've learned *outside*, it's that you have to strike back immediately. Mental karate. The Smetana Theatre was more appropriate, I had seen ballet performances there even as a child. The Smetana Theatre next to the train station was originally called the

New German Theatre—a response to the Czech National Theatre, which burned shortly before its opening in 1881; hardly two years later it was reopened, with help from the whole country, all the villages and towns pitched in. The National Theatre itself was a response to the German Estates Theatre, where *Don Giovanni* was first performed. The history of the city is a history of responses between Czechs and Germans, without either side ever asking a question.

Vyšehrad. Here stood the palace of the Bohemian kings and queens, destroyed in the 15$^{th}$ century by Hussites. Here the Czechs didn't even ask the Czechs a question.

Hundreds of years before that, under Charles IV, this is where the coronation train had started, before processing through the New Town, the Old Town, and Malá Strana, up to the castle, along the Royal Way. Now you can only see the baroque fortifications, brick work; the oldest part, a rotunda, was intermittently used as a powder magazine.

I go to the cemetery. This is where Smetana and Dvořák are buried, and Purkyně, Mácha, Neruda, and Čapek, Němcová—where can you get cowslips in December? The cemetery of honor is empty, no one is interested in the national past. Tourists hardly recognize the names.

In the park outside, pensioners are feeding sparrows, a kindergarten class walks together, holding a rope, and from her pedestal, Libuše prophecies the glory of the city. From Horymír's cliff I see the Vltava under me with the railway bridge. This is where the imprisoned Horymír is said to have escaped execution by jumping from the cliff with his horse. *Nuže Šemíku, vzhůru!* Come on, Šemík, up! Most of Vyšehrad is legend, myth. The most convincing thing about it is the silence. The wind picks up.

I go back to the Nusle Bridge. Under construction for nine years, it was opened in 1974 after a bunch of tanks were sent across as a load test. On top is a six-lane road, the north-south highway connecting Prague 2, Vinohrady, with

Prague 4, Pankrác; underneath, the metro runs through the body of the bridge. The bridge is a scant half a kilometer long, forty meters above the Nusle valley. Below me I see the streets and back courtyards, altered by annexes planned as provisional accommodation and never taken down. It's drafty here, and looking down makes me dizzy. I feel the vibrations when cars drive by. The rusty railings are painted with "God does not love suicides" and "Remember that you're not alone."

Long ago the paper *Večerní Praha*, "Evening Prague," ran a story about the Nusle Bridge: "Sad statistic: As of 1 pm on July 25, 1990, 152 people have ended their lives by jumping from this bridge, from the Prague 2 side as well as from our side, the Prague 4 police reported (hats off, Prague 4!; Prague 2: no comment). Of these, 102 had been men and 50 women. Only one suicide jumped in 1974, while 1986 was the year with the most suicides: seventeen cases. The majority—nearly two thirds of the suicides—had chosen the half of the bridge over Prague 2. As for the motives, 92 cases suffered from health or mental problems, while twelve jumpers were looking to escape problems at work. Nine suicides had emotional reasons, eight had family reasons, and in five cases, it was incurable alcoholics who ended their lives. In 26 cases the reason for the suicide could not be determined."

I look around. There are no pedestrians, only a man with a briefcase on the other side of the street, above the gas station, where most Prague 2 jumpers jump; it's already changed owners. Does one jump with one's briefcase, or leave it behind? And why jump over a gas station? He's already turned off, towards Vinohrady. I look down at the pavement in Nusle. Ugliness could also be a reason. One hundred fifty-two. By now, at the end of 1992, the number must have reached a hundred seventy, especially considering how rapidly the conditions for older people are worsening. The undetermined cases must include all the pensioners pushed by bored youths.

The reasons remain, only the labels are new. Before, when the bridge was called the Klement Gottwald Bridge, people hadn't argued with God. Maybe back then police patrolled here instead. Now they're nowhere to be found in the city when you need them.

I turn left, toward Albertov, past the octagon of St. Charles church, which Charles IV had built in the style of the cathedral in Aachen where Charlemagne is buried. It's part of a former Benedictine monastery, which now houses a portion of the state archives, while the other half contains the Police Museum. I'm freezing, and it's open.

A school class is just leaving, they're excited, the children are laughing. In a special exhibition on "Unusual Criminal Cases" there's no mention of the dead from the bridge, only of someone who executed himself with a homemade guillotine. A tinkerer: the device is described in great detail with all the technical specifications; he had used it for years to split firewood. The guestbook is full of appreciative entries. The museum is empty. The woman at the ticket desk is pleased that someone else has come. Please sign in, she says. We need fifteen visitors per day; the teachers don't like to bring their students, and otherwise we have to close.

The Benedictines must be trying to reclaim the place. Now the church is even making claims on the cathedral in Hradčany. It's a national treasure, I've learned. I sign in twice, with different names and addresses; only the round, retrograde script of the second address is fake.

Even the earlier Museum of National State Security didn't get a lot of visitors. School classes, sporadically; no one came voluntarily except for a few lost tourists. The population's innate mistrust of the police, regardless of which regime they served. But the museum was actually quite fascinating: guns confiscated from spies, secret agents, and saboteurs stared from the wall, their barrels aimed threateningly at visitors. There were 444 of them from 1952 alone. In the first room, the period from 1918–1945, gendarmerie carbines and three heavy machine guns: "Masaryk let the workers be shot at" had been a dictum of the Communists, who themselves had quashed every strike. In the hall of "Martial Glory," banners of the border guards, in further rooms, the legend of the "Victory of the Working Populace in February 1948"; the subsequent exponential expansion of the Ministry of the Interior's troops and the National Security Corps. The people's militias that carried out the coup, the "Fighting Fist of the Working Class," continued to be equipped until the eighties, with missiles even. A hall dedicated to the Ninth Party Congress of the Communist Party of Czechoslovakia, next to it one about the international cooperation of the security corps of the Socialist countries, with copies of relevant documents, signatures, photographs—pieces of evidence. The name KGB appeared nowhere. The confiscated printing press that produced counterfeit Czechoslovakian banknotes was impressive; for that currency, nothing but a waste of talent and idealism. In a vitrine, an unused diving suit, torn off the body of someone attempting to flee the GDR through Czechoslovakia. An exhibition of artworks dedicated to the National Security Corps from the Czech and Slovak Endowment for the Fine Arts; all well-known names. The highpoint: the successful German shepherd, an assistant border guard, who caught a record number of saboteurs and spies, stuffed on a pedestal.

Visitors had to don slippers made of felt and green military cloth and conduct themselves with dignity. I could never convince any of my acquaintances to go.

The concept of the new Police Museum is harmless by contrast. The only interesting thing is a letter of safe conduct from an 18th century nobleman, a travel document. In addition to body measurements and age, one could tell from certain flourishes of the handwriting, letter variants, paper quality, and ornamentation, that the person in question was a French diplomat partial to plants and alcohol, sickly, unhappily in love, melancholic, financially secure, a smoker. The system of ciphers was apparently known to the police in all European countries.

More recent history is less elegant; the exhibits that have been kept are not nearly as interesting as those from before 1989. No more agitation, no saboteurs, the gun barrels have disappeared from the walls. Instead there are games for children about traffic rules. A large two-part plywood map with differently-colored lights representing police stations of various significance throughout the republic; Slovakia is already removable.

At the end came a single picture. November 17, 1989: on one side the police, on the other, students; the young people handing flowers to the masked police behind their plexiglass shields, their clubs raised. No commentary.

I leave. Meanwhile dusk has fallen, it's snowing. St. Charles church is open, the interior is dark, only the octagonal star vault sparkles weakly, reflecting the lights from outside. A crèche has been set up in the Bethlehem Chapel next to the altar, sparsely lit with candles, as now for Christmas in all of the churches; one of the three kings lies in the hay, the donkey and sheep in the stable are newly carved. An old woman kneels, murmuring, before a side altar. She looks up briefly to see whether I cross myself. I leave her to it. Outside the snow has picked up.

I walk past St. Apollinaire, where alcoholics are brought to dry out, next to the Villa "Amerika" with the Antonín Dvořák museum. The gate in the wrought-iron fence is closed, and I don't want to look at any music now anyway.

I notice that I move differently than the pedestrians around me. They walk faster, with shopping bags, bundled up, they're in a hurry to get home from work. A brief, burning jealousy, every time I'm here. I know there's no idyll behind the lit windowpanes but I always let myself be seduced by the normality, the everyday worries that I don't share. When I meet acquaintances, we envy each other: they me for my freedom, I them for their bondage.

At the quayside I take the tram, the 17 is just arriving.

As ever, the swimming stadium is open until ten o'clock in the evening. "It's been a long time, miss," says the cloak-room attendant as she gives me the locker key. I recognize her too; years ago I was here every day. The other attendant is new. "Or should I rather say young lady?" "As you like," I laugh.

The lockers are narrower than they were before, they've fit in twice as many now. I go to the showers, stand under the stream for a long time, as always, letting the water run over my head, gradually becoming warm. Then into the cold-water tub, it takes some willpower. Then to the outdoor pools. For now I don't go in the indoor pool at all: too warm, too chlorinated, too full. In the smaller pool outside people are playing water polo, the other is almost empty, only three lanes are occupied. I get in, it's always the same joy: the return to the primordial element. I swim a few laps and then turn on my back. The stars above me, barely visible. Betelgeuze. Snow falls into my eyes. The sky is releasing flakes nonstop, they melt on my face, I taste them cool on my lips.

With bleached eyes I climb out after half an hour, slip on the wet tiles, snow is already sticking on the grass. I go briefly into the hall, the big pool is emptying out, the last swimmers continue unhindered, a few young men sit on the steps, a group of girls in front of them who keep turning around and giggling. I just wanted to see it again.

"Hey, it's Nora!" The lifeguard comes toward me, in white pants and a white shirt. I don't recognize him immediately. Yes, Lena and Lea in school, Nora to the others. I was spared the official name Leonora, it was only later that it stopped alienating me. He has a belly, gray hair, seems jovial. "You haven't been here in ages!" I think he must be able to see in my face how long it's been, but he looks at my figure, as is usual here. Maybe I'm wearing the old bathing suit that I wore here night after night, I don't remember when I bought a new one. I see him helping keep the beginners above water with a pole. We've never really talked, only nodded to each other. Now he's telling me that he's going skiing with his grandkids next week and hopes the snow will hold out.

I go down the slippery steps to the showers, first to the steam room. The sauna is already closed, but the steam room is part of the pool facilities. It's particularly hot today. I squeeze onto the bench, I can hardly see the others. It stings in my nose, my skin burns with every movement. As the room empties, I stretch out on my towel, accidentally touching two women next to me; I can tell that they're sweating much more than I. As if everything in me were slow, my metabolism, my whole development. The ceiling drips, steam hisses out of a pipe, the little stalactites were here twenty years ago, they've surely been chipped off in the meantime. I close my eyes. After a while I feel someone touching my shoulder. "Excuse me, but you've been in here quite a while." I stand up. A woman, younger than me, motherly, is bending over me. The scar on her belly is right in front of my face. I obey. Thank you, I stand up. I'm dizzy. I open the door, stagger to the tub, I shudder at the icy water but when I emerge I feel good. I spray myself off with the hose and go to the changing rooms. Women stand in front of the wall of mirrors, drying their hair under pipes that blow warm air. I see their bodies. They compare themselves, humorously, without envy. There are some slim ones, athletic, mostly under twenty. Then the bellies and thighs start to develop. After the evening swim under falling snow, the faces are smooth, relaxed, friendly. In the showers, too—lending shampoo and soap is taken for granted. Women among themselves, their readiness to help. I like them all. "I'd like to be that slim," one says, looking at me. I'm pleased. The day wasn't wasted.

Not too much despair, not too much emptiness.

3.

A stack of forgotten newspapers from the summer.

There's a frog museum in Switzerland. In Estavayer-le-Lac in Canton Fribourg; the collection owes its existence to "one pensioner's battle against boredom." In 1849 François Perrier, a pensioned officer of the Swiss Guards, returned from the Vatican to his birthplace. Having nothing to do, he prowled the banks of Lake Neuchâtel, searching for frogs. Not to eat them, but to stuff them. In an odd panopticon, one hundred eight of these amphibians present the social life of the nineteenth century. In three vitrines, visitors can see a family dinner, a round of cards, a school class with a pupil kneeling for punishment before the teacher, a barber shop, a trial, a banquet. The highpoint: a military exercise, observed by a frog invalid with a wooden leg. Fifteen thousand visitors per year, including tourists from America and East Asia, come to look at the frogs. Most are sad, like the museum's employees, that after the sudden death of the author of these scenes at age forty-eight, no one had managed to pick up where his originality left off.

Thirty years later the postman Cheval began realizing his dreams in the form of idiosyncratic termite mounds: nuggets glued together as if with secretions: stones, shells, branches, roots, mosses, all covered with a gray compound which then hardened. It took him thirty-three years to build. He left his neighbors, who ridiculed him, messages on tablets and scraps of paper, didn't have it in him to actually talk to them, he'd grown shy over the years of his strained search for form, only held mumbled conversations with himself. He held up his work before the farmers as proof of his industriousness, he didn't see himself as an artist: *Hereux l'homme libre brave et travailleur. Le reve d'un Paysan.*

His temples, grottoes, and labyrinths suggest Bomarzo. The pensioned Swiss Guardsman with his frogs suggests Switzerland. Twenty years later Adolf Wölfli began condensing his imaginations into an odd universe of violent word objects, drawings, and musical scores in Waldau near Bern: dissections: inside the head of a solipsist; greetings to Cheval.

The dolphins of the Soviet Navy undergo a "conversion to civilian use":

The Black Sea dolphin Diana pulls a small child after it, swimming safely past the nets to the spot where it's usually thrown a herring. Soon it receives no more herrings at the base.

At the height of military tensions several dozen dolphins were kept in a secret saltwater aquarium near Sevastopol, trained to protect against enemy divers and to search for mines and torpedos.

If we don't get some assistance soon we'll be forced to sell the dolphins to the circus, says Anton Pugovkin, who's been a trainer for twenty years. We're on the edge of the abyss. Once we had a powerful navy behind us, now we're only a poor government agency; soon we won't even be able to feed the animals. When the secret program was in its heyday, we had up to seventy dolphins here, he reminisces. Equipped with special vests and distress rockets, deployed in the protective corridor in front of docking stations, not to kill enemy divers or to install mines—he and the others could only laugh at that idea. Theoretically a dolphin is clever enough to launch an atomic bomb, Pugovkin says. But it's not strong enough to carry a mine, even if we wanted it to. The new Ukrainian navy isn't rich enough to pay for dolphins to search for expensive weaponry that got lost in the ocean in test exercises. Not even the Russian-commanded Black Sea Fleet, the subject of squabbles between Moscow and the Ukraine, could think up any military use for the mammals. Diana, one of six remaining dolphins, is used to help children overcome phobias: neuroses, nightmares, and bedwetting are successfully treated here; some of the children are barely two years old. The trainer looks at his highly specialized dolphins with some disappointment: they hadn't gone to all this trouble just for them to splash around with children.

Years ago in the old Prague Police Museum: the retired museum guide reports with disgust that some of the police dogs had been duds as well. So much time squandered, food costs down the drain; it was supposed to catch saboteurs, instead this expensive specialized dog was wallowing in a sandbox with children. It couldn't even be used as a watch-dog. All the best training and nothing but a disappointment.

I think of dogs, weaker than dolphins, deployed in war with mines on their backs, under their bellies, trained to crawl underneath low vehicles and tanks, the explosives were set off remotely. The Russians rarely cared about animals, just as they rarely cared about people.

Nonetheless, they withdrew.

Now there's even documentation.

The negotiations were tough. The Russians had their tactics for wearing down opponents: getting them drunk, intimidating them with brotherly embraces, kisses, slogans of friendship. In October 1968, after the occupation, the Czechoslovakian delegation returned from the Soviet Union with humiliating conditions for the "temporary presence of Soviet troops in the ČSSR": "We can roll over you in a few hours. Do you want peace and quiet, or a bloodbath? We won't see the Soviet Army insulted!" The soldiers must have been deeply affected by the leaflets with which Prague was blanketed overnight: "Ivan, go home! Your Natasha is with Kolya, the deserter."

Times change. *They won't shout us down*, wrote one of the negotiators. The first meeting took place in mid-January 1990, a month after the first official note, and after repeated warnings from Prague. The Russians played for time. Still, they'd never been so quickly brought to the bargaining table, it was a unique occurrence in Soviet diplomacy. After the upheavals of November 1989, the new Czechoslovak Foreign Minister took office. Like the other politicians of the Civic Forum, who came straight from prison or from washing dishes, he had little experience with day-to-day bureaucracy. He called in the old deputy, long-practiced in appeasement: Mr. Deputy, *pane náměstku,* you're sixty, retirement age. Either you prepare and execute the negotiations honestly, so that they succeed—in which case I'll send you somewhere to be ambassador for two years—or you make a mistake, play both sides, and retire immediately. The deputy, a professional, accepted. At first, next to other platitudes, he referred to the leader of the Soviet delegation as "my friend Aboimov," but that was soon resolved. The Russians came directly to their base in Milovice on a special plane without finding it necessary to report the flyover; they rejected accommodations in Prague and arrived at the talks by military bus.

A group of people in civilian clothes and thirty officers of the rank of General or Colonel versus fifteen negotiators on the Czech side, mostly civilians: lawyers, engineers.

First the military rejected every concrete definition of the object and purpose of the talks, claiming to have no mandate. The initial negotiations were over what was to be negotiated. Most of the Russians seemed surprised to be understood as an occupying power, not to be well-liked in the country. The word "withdrawal" was a red rag to all; the Russians were not prepared to go beyond "incremental reduction of armed forces in Central Europe," contingent on negotiations in Vienna, which had already been dragging on for two years. The Czechs insisted that these were to be bilateral talks, independent of the maneuvering of the major powers in Vienna, revising the treaties that had been imposed in 1968 after the invasion: nullifying them. In this way it became clear how poorly informed they were about the activities of Soviet troops on their own territory. They knew neither exact numbers nor how they were equipped nor what they were constantly drilling for. In the operational plans of the Soviet leadership, Czech territory was planned as scorched earth from the beginning. In the case of an attack, the Czech army was to advance to the Rhine, cross a three-hundred-kilometer-wide section of it, and then cease to exist: in the sixties river crossings were repeatedly practiced in "Vltava" maneuvers. Conversely, should the armies of the Warsaw Pact be forced to retreat, the square of Bohemia was to be surrendered and the first line of defense established further east, on the Moravian border.

During the negotiations the Soviets threatened several times to break off the talks entirely, they haggled over every word. Should it be "including," "*včetně*," включая, or *v tom čisle*? Once they were finally able to talk about a *withdrawal*, the real problems came out. Before that, the Russians had brought up a string of treaties and agreements that the Soviet Union, in the pursuit of security, had concluded since the thirties at every international meeting and on all levels: on the inviolability of borders, the honoring of foreign territory, non-aggression pacts—including the statutes of the Warsaw Pact on collective defense—never on collective attack.

Because of the technical challenges involved, it would take ten years to remove all military equipment and personnel, the Soviets claimed. They deemed the Czech demand that they be withdrawn by the end of the year unrealistic, but in the next round of talks they came down to five years. Eighteen hundred trains would be necessary for the transport of materials alone, that meant two years; the limited capacity of the transfer station at Čierna pri Čope meant it couldn't manage more than two or three trains a day. Now that the Russians were finally naming numbers, the

Czechs were able to calculate that eight hundred trains would suffice, and that it would take six to seven months. Commitments and assurances from the railway union flooded in from throughout the republic: they would load seven trains a day, as long as those trains were filled with Soviet troops. And to keep trains from backing up over the border, the Czechoslovak army offered to build the Soviets a new loading station in three weeks, with their track gauge; the Russians claimed that would take another year. Finally they came out with the real reason: a portion of the transport goods, seventeen hundred special artillery shells, required special handling. Therefore, it would take significantly longer. —Contrary to all official statements that they had no nuclear weapons in Europe outside their own territory, the Soviets had been storing nuclear warheads on Czechoslovak land the whole time.

The second round of talks took place a month later in Moscow. Yet more soldiers. Now that the technical problems had been discussed, in the civil committees the main issue was finally put on the table: they didn't know where to put the people—there were no barracks for the seventy-five thousand soldiers, and no apartments for the seventeen thousand officers' families. They had never imagined actually having to withdraw; the occupation had been planned for all eternity, like their steadfast friendship. The high Soviet functionary made this confession in the expectation that the Czech side would have understanding for such humanitarian problems. One of the negotiators, the historian Jaroslav Šedivý, finally lost his patience. Mr. Deputy, *pane náměstku*, we've had your humanitarian problems for twenty years, since you took these apartments away from our people.

The military became direct: You're going to beg us to come back when the Germans overrun you. Why are large-scale American maneuvers being carried out right now in

Bavaria, of all places? And who's going to buy all your goods after we're gone?

Even during the negotiations, the number of trains that had been rolling eastward out of Czechoslovakia for decades, sealed against tampering, stuffed full of textiles and supplies, rose noticeably. An exchange rate of 1:30 was arranged for the Soviet army, at a time when the official rate was 1:9 and the tourist rate 1:12—both already criminally inflated assessments of the value of the ruble. Two thirds of all expenditures by the occupying troops were covered by the Czechoslovak state. Haggling over tariffs and compensation for soil damage would have caused further delays, so it was largely dispensed with. Parallel to all this, a rock singer and member of parliament had founded a subcommittee to monitor the withdrawal and had personally negotiated with a group of Soviet representatives; thus the talks were assured of support from the media and amongst the public.

At the end came a final official plea from Gorbachev, who had delayed making a clear condemnation of the '68 occupation until the last possible moment, asking that the withdrawal proceed within two years instead of by year's end, for humanitarian reasons. Havel agreed to eighteen months. The Czech side had informed Hungary; the Russians were about to go through the same negotiations in Budapest. Western countries reacted with little understanding: England, arrogant since Munich '38 wherever Czechoslovakia was concerned, reproved the Czechs, saying that they'd negatively influenced the disarmament talks by going it alone. The withdrawal of British troops from West Germany was concluded two years later.

The last Soviet soldier left Czechoslovakia on June 30, 1991, a few days before the deadline. They just couldn't understand why no one came to bid them farewell.

Images from Milovice after the withdrawal. Left behind: a lumpish Lenin made of cast concrete, filthy barracks without windows, the wooden planks ripped out, broken, oil-contaminated earth.

But they're gone.

Nowhere else did it go that fast.

Before I let my breast swell with pride, I look at the other newspapers. Three special editions of the *Uncensored Newspaper* from summer 1992, each over sixty pages thick, with four-column lists of employees of the StB, the secret police, divided into "foreign handlers," "providers of safehouses," "agents," "secret collaborators," and "persons of trust": one hundred fourteen names per column. I leaf through indifferently, at first uninterested, until I start to see names I know: actors, popular singers, artists, and journalists, but also neighbors, professors.

A busy columnist, known for his "sharp pen," active in theater companies for German tourists, *Culture as joint venture*, listed twice as "Alex": years of efficient collaboration.

Unsurprising: an assistant professor in the German Studies department, included in the list of handlers as "Vladimir," already onerous during my studies, surpassed in denunciatory zeal only by the East German editor "Sieglinde." The others had turned a blind eye.

The New Zealander "Ian," former KGB agent, hiding out as an English lecturer in Czechoslovakia after being exposed. Another unpleasant memory from my college days.

The agile literary critic "Rosa," retired Marxist, responsible since her student days in the fifties for destroying the careers of fellow students and professors. The party had shaped private lives as well: her younger sister, an insecure painter, was married off to a "wonderful comrade" and taken in by the Party Academy, where she was put in charge of the noticeboard. After '68 "Rosa" had felt persecuted as a reform Communist. She subsisted in a private apartment near the castle. Now at seventy she's back at it, disseminating her standards of Socialist realism through art criticism, and her reviews get published. The aggrieved generation of '68 is making its presence felt, while the political prisoners of the fifties, the camp survivors and members of the Resistance, the old, with destroyed lives and rotten health, wait with resignation for some kind of reparation. Most are dead, forgotten.

The president had distanced himself from the publication of the lists, sharply condemned the disclosure of names; there could be cases of mistaken identity, injustice, tragic entanglements, he said. The newspaper answered that the president surrounded himself with dubious staff members, politically tainted persons, and his so-called advisors were all amateurs without the necessary knowledge and capabilities. This accusation was repeated in other newspapers, accompanied by examples. The president's spokesperson had himself perpetrated several gross outrages in press conferences, even toward foreign journalists; he was no longer sustainable due to his arrogant incompetence and was given an ambassadorship in the USA. There he would be equally incompetent, but less visible. In an interview, he was asked about his work: "I endeavor to convince persons of note in American business and politics to grace our republic with a visit." Such sycophancy hadn't been seen even under the Russians, the newspaper commented.

The president's maneuvering was criticized: instead of attending to internal problems, he travelled the world, everyone's darling, *from dissident to president*, from America to Israel, and privately to the Bahamas as well. Played the mediator in the Near East while the problems piled up at home. He shouldn't be surprised if matters in Slovakia came to a head.

I think of this polite man, trying to remain friendly to everyone everywhere.

Dissidenting is an art too, the newspaper wrote. Where are all those who aren't protected by their famous names, who spent years in prison being raped by their Roma cellmates, being abused by sadistic kapos and wardens, the unknowns who had put up with more and got no visits from Mitterand for their pains, no celebrity? Who will close Europe's longest red-light district, the E55, the main road to Germany, where the pimps of Polish, Russian, and Albanian women wage war against each other in the casinos while outside the prostitutes have to drum up business in all weather, the gypsies who don't know whether their children will become Czechs or Slovaks?

This too is my country.

There was something else. That can't be all.

A fellow student, a Spaniard. Grew up in an industrial city in North Bohemia; his father, a Communist, expelled from Spain with others from the Party after the civil war. Austria was too bourgeois for him, it had to be Bohemia, a pokey town in the provinces so that they wouldn't settle in, the kids either. At some point they were going back. The son learned the new language quickly.

He spoke several languages, was well-read. After his studies he got a job as an editor at a publishing house. He translated for his circle of friends from Spanish and French: nothing controversial—philosophy, sociology. The group was deemed conspiratorial; his language skills made him suspicious to the StB. He was locked up for nine months, then worked briefly as a night watchman at the metalworking plant ZUKOV in Prague-Holešovice. There one night Jan Palach's memorial plaque was melted down after being confiscated by the police. The retired woman who was on duty was sent home. The bronze was still warm when he arrived at his shift.

His time in prison changed him. He grew unsociable, aggressive, isolated.

While his friends pursued careers, he couldn't manage to capitalize on his past.

He had peculiar qualities:

He got a tapeworm from the Spanish vegetables his father grew in an allotment garden, a kind previously unknown in Bohemia, something Mediterranean.

In the Vltava he found a piece of moldavite, a semi-precious stone that hadn't been seen for ages in the turbid flood waters: a shard formed from a meteorite's impact.

He found a pearl in a tin of mussels.

Finally, bees came to him. A whole swarm built combs under his window in the old town, beautiful white clusters of wax. He was the only one in the street with a flowerpot on his windowsill.

Another fellow student I was close to once is a taciturn sculptor who has been working on making the same objects in the same chockablock studio for years. The variations are minimal. At one time he would open his studio, make coffee, talk about films. Now the door remains closed, and there's a gate across the building's entryway.

I fold up the newspapers, absorbing words: *conversion*, *dislocation*, *harmonogram*, *ravaged*.

A story from the recent past is only now coming to light.

(ČTK) The Russian army, "heir to the glorious martial heritage" of its universally feared Soviet predecessor, is today only a shadow of that powerful, celebrated, privileged, spoiled, armed-to-the-teeth colossus.

Barely three months ago classmates and friends sent off quiet, smiling Mischa Kubarski from the mid-Russian town of Yaroslavl to do his military service. They wished him a tolerable tour and a speedy return. He was back by spring—

in a zinc coffin. He had served in a tank battalion not far from Khabarovsk in the Far East. Private Mikhail Kubarski died of starvation.

Much remains unclear in this tragic case. During the aforementioned three months, Kubarski underwent three medical examinations: one upon conscription, another at the beginning of his tour, and a third "in-depth examination" shortly before his death, when all soldiers in his unit were examined by a medical commission from the district army hospital. Diagnosis: apparently healthy. Eighteen days after this "in-depth check," Soldier Kubarski came to the clinic complaining of weakness. It was determined that he was dramatically underweight—in concrete terms, he weighed twelve kilos less than the medically recommended minimum for his age and body mass. The commander of the medical service, Major Sirchenko, found "nothing worrisome" about the soldier's condition; nonetheless, he sent him to the hospital in Khabarovsk, 50 km away. The unit's ambulance had been slated for repairs for half a year; Kubarski took the bus. He collapsed during the journey.

Two days after his death, an army medical inspector descended on the battalion and immediately admitted over fifty soldiers to the hospital. Diagnosis—"severe malnutrition."

Emaciated soldiers wolfed down the judiciously-sized portions of barley porridge with butter and borscht and shuddered thinking of the moment when they would have to return to their unit. There they often got nothing more than warmed-over cabbage for a week at a time, and they didn't see bread for days on end.

The army basically lived on credit.

The magazine *Reflex* shows the winning images from the World Press Photo contest. First prize in the category "Daily Life": a photo by the Russian photographer Ivan Kurtov.

Four sailors stand at attention on a Leningrad quay, saluting a highly-decorated veteran naval officer who rolls past them on a skateboard, legless. *Keep smiling, boys!* The city in the background is hardly recognizable through the smog.

I imagine a dolphin with the rank of major carrying a bald child from Chernobyl on its back. The environmental damage in the Soviet Union is worse than all comparable destruction elsewhere in the world put together. By these standards the spectacular Greenpeace protests on oil rigs and nuclear test atolls look like private acrobatics shows.

In the American army, dogs were also decorated. In the pet cemetery near Raleigh, North Carolina: "War dog, U.S. Army, Honorable Discharge: Jigger, 3-7-40—9-26-53." Often a portrait of a German shepherd on the gravestone, and an American flag on the ground next to it. Are there dogs in Arlington too? I didn't see any dog graves at the National Cemetery in Chatanooga. There's a penguin in Raleigh as well: "Pandora Pekok, penguin, best friend and confidant, 1972–1989." No rank. The Chinese emperor Qin Shi Huang, famous for the spectacular terracotta army that was to watch over his tomb after his death, and for his lifelong search for the elixir of immortality, conferred ranks on trees and hills. A hill was clearcut and razed because it blocked his view. A tree that had once sheltered him from rain was appointed "Minister of the Fifth Rank." The builders and artists that constructed his tomb were not allowed to leave it, and were buried in its walls alive.

The delusions of the mighty are reality for the weak.


I'm already somewhere else.

In *Gravity's Rainbow* Thomas Pynchon sketches a biographical paradigm. One of the most ludicrous stories describes efforts to bring literacy to the Turkic peoples in the early Stalin era. Vaslav Tchitcherine, special envoy from the Cultural Committee in Moscow, transferred for disciplinary reasons to the Seven Rivers region, tries to introduce the NTA, the New Turkic Alphabet, thereby getting into a bitter struggle with his rival Igor Blobadjian "from the prestigious G Committee," who wishes to appropriate Tchitcherine's "uvular plosive" (another kind of G). One day all the chairs for Tschitcherine's meeting have been sawed through, and two dozen linguists land on the ground. In revenge, Tschitcherine translates the first sura of the Koran into the proposed NTA and has it circulated amongst the Arabists, who are very sensitive about any profanation, under the name of Igor Blobadjian. This undreamt-of outrage causes Blobadjian, who can't explain what's happened, to be pursued by scimitar-waving Arabists into the darkest corner of Baku, through abandoned oil derricks, chambers, sheds, pipes. Blobadjian flees without knowing whither, the pursuers on his heels; the last hatch falls shut.

This way! What is this? You're no part of this anymore. Your journey leads elsewhere. It's time. You're already in another tunnel. Go.

**4.**

In the morning I open the apartment door, startling a cat who was crouching on the top step as if on the lookout. I call to it and it scurries past me, won't be pet. It's red. I stifle the impulse to run after it. It must belong to someone from downstairs, I've seen it in the building a few times. It's shy, as if it were half wild or I a stranger here. I never had a red cat. Three times I had a black one, with a white spot on the throat, two striped ones—one with a pattern like a clouded leopard—and a white one, as a child. It was a beast.

It would be nice to have someone, actually—an animal waiting for me, but not here, not in this apartment that doesn't belong to me. There's a plant here, left by my predecessor. I descend upon it immediately and water it without realizing that it hardly needs water after all this time, and if it does, then only in small doses. In my zeal, my need to see things to rights here, as if I could justify my presence with solicitousness, I destroy the plant. I find a stick while out walking on Petřín and tie the plant to it; one branch is drooping under the weight of the leaves and threatening to break. I search the apartment for twine and find children's books; I'd had some of the same ones, in more carefully-selected editions, hardcover, with ribbon bookmarks. These are laminated with plastic, the illustrations are rude simplifications of the old pictures. I read through a few fairy tales. The texts are simplified as well: condensed, retold, without glamour, without mystery.

Looking at these sticky, grubby books, forgotten under clutter like the plant, I ask myself again what it is I'm doing here. When I water the plant or try, with a broken vacuum cleaner, to make the apartment a little more home-like, my actions resemble something staged. I drown a plant and feel useful, while others in the house pick up children from kindergarten or school, lug groceries in string bags—the old shopping nets filled with vegetables, meat, fish, and oil, picked up after the end of a long working day in crowded shops; the lines at checkout. I see them carrying Christmas trees, repairing sleds, forcing hats, scarves, and mittens on children.

They live directly in clean copy without trying anything first, while I'm still crossing through the first draft on scratch paper. The old outline for school essays: introduction, body, conclusion. Sometimes I feel as if I must be long-since in the body, but really I'm still scribbling away at the introduction, still drafting. Everything has to be right; I have so many requirements I never make it to the theme. Life—as they say. I just can't grasp the fact that this is it.

The cat is gone. There's a draft in the stairwell, cold air that carries the smell of coal, and silvery particles—hoarfrost that's drifted down from the roof; the hatch is open on the top floor. I go up; the chain that closes the hatch is hooked, there should be a ladder on the wall, but it's missing. I think about whether I could ring one of the doorbells, but I don't know anyone here. Mornings mostly only pensioners are home—old women, suspicious, they have no ladders or can no longer carry them; most probably wouldn't open the door anyway.

I'm turning back when I see a bird on the cupboard in the hallway, a blackbird, crouching on the edge, frozen or injured, the wind must have brought it in. That's why the cat's here. I come closer, lift my hand, think about what I could catch it with. The bird flutters and backs up close to the wall where I can't reach it. I fumble toward it while one eye watches me, the lid half closed. As soon as I'm within the critical distance, it hops up and evades my grasp. I've forgotten that it actually disgusts me: the mite-covered feathers, as on the hundred thousand pigeons in the city. I come from the other side, touch it. It flies up to the hatch but doesn't make it through, the opening is too narrow. The snow is coming in on gusts of wind now, it's already dusted one step and I can feel my fingers getting stiff with cold. The bird flutters between cupboard and ceiling, crashes into the hatch, and lands on the floor but flies up again as soon as I approach. I see it clearly now. It's bigger than a blackbird, and its head is different. The wings are black with red stripes—it's not a blackbird. I know of blackbirds with white speckles, variants I observed in Frankfurt, partial albinos that weren't accepted by the others and were left to fend for themselves when the crows came.

I've seen this bird before, but not in Europe. Red and black—the robins in New York have a red throat and a red belly, but no stripes on the wings. It was a barren place—abandoned, treeless; I was surprised when the bird sang. Now I know where it was. Masada.

A plateau, Herod's fortress on top: the remains of defense walls, citadels, and palaces, steep, dizzying slopes. A rock desert at the foot of the Dead Sea, the old "asphalt sea," the water so bitterly salty that it burns the eyes and mouth, the bird sang to the besieged: Tristan, Tristram—black and red. The last Jews who resisted the Romans; three years after the conquest of Jerusalem, a community of barely a thousand against a military power ten times stronger, for seven months. They had more to eat and drink than the besiegers, they hoped to starve them out; the cisterns were full of water, the stocks of grain, oil, and dates stored up by Herod had kept for nearly a hundred years in the dry air and would have sufficed for several years more. Herod had had the fortress expanded into a refuge from his Jewish foes, who didn't see him as the rightful successor to King David, and from the great danger—that Cleopatra would march on Judea. The upper plateau, six hundred fifty meters long, three hundred meters wide, with two palaces, baths, administrative buildings, dwellings, and magazines, was encircled by a wall with defense towers; the biggest one stood on the rock spur in the west, where a neighboring mountain was the closest thing to the summit.

The night before the fall of Masada the Jews destroyed everything except their stores of food and water, so the victors didn't think they had killed themselves for profane reasons—960 men, women, and children. They drew lots: ten men were to kill the others, then one was to kill the other nine. Afterwards, after they'd set fire to the houses, to the Northern Palace and the Western Palace, the baths—the Roman bath and the *mikveh*, the ritual bath—to the temple, the arsenals, the *columbarium*, where once, during the first Roman occupation, pigeons had been raised, the last man killed himself. The Masada lottery.

Some had doubts. Not everyone wanted to die, to let their families, wives, and children be slaughtered; enslavement to the Romans was not more terrible than living and dying with their tribesmen.

The long speech by the commander Eleazar ben Ya'ir: *Brave and loyal followers!* The vicissitudes of euphoria and deepest despair; in the end, the wind decided.

The Romans had erected a siege ramp from the western side of the nearest mountain, along which they'd run a battering ram and broken through the massive watchtower, then tried to destroy the defense wall built by the city's inhabitants as well. The wall was built of wood and earth heaped up between two rows of cross-braced timbers, the ram was powerless—the earth was just packed harder with each blow. After long, fruitless attempts, the Romans finally put burning torches to the wall. The wall caught fire. But the wind turned, coming now from the northwest and forcing the fire back on the Romans; the ballistae, the shields, and the ropes began to burn. They were about to retreat—the city would wait for days and weeks, but the fire wouldn't—the mountain was surrounded. But then the wind changed again. Now it came from the southeast, blowing toward the wall. The wall burned to the ground. The Romans knew that on the next day, Masada would be theirs. They withdrew to their camp and waited for morning.

The decision was made in the night. At first, Eleazar did not have all the men on his side. Neither his Sicarii—named for their daggers, "sicae,"—who had plundered the plains by the Dead Sea for years and caused more bloodbaths among the Jews than among the stationed Romans, nor the Zealots, the "eager," who had holed up with them at Masada, were immediately taken in by his words.

Eleazar turned now to the hesitant ones. God, who made the wind change, was reminding them of their misdeeds—he was turning away. All that remained to fulfill God's will for his once dear people was death at their own hands: "For if he had continued to bless us, or were only slightly angry at us, he would not have stood back and calmly watched the downfall of so many . . . I was much deceived when I thought I was fighting alongside brave men!"

That's how he convinced the men. No one asked the women.

Two women hid themselves and five children in an underground water pipe and survived. When the Romans came the next day, they told them what had happened. Thus could Eleazar's speech be written down and the decision preserved as a historical act. Otherwise the Sicarii would have gone down in history only as plunderers, if they had been remembered at all; now, they are known for their heroism: "Let our wives die unabused, our children without knowledge of slavery!" —Through the testimony of two unheroic women who did not submit to the madness of their sect and did not allow themselves to be slaughtered.

The bird looks at me like I'm a murderer. My attempts at rescue are driving it wild. I grasp it and it pecks at me, flutters, loses a feather. I wanted to set it free from my apartment window, but now I've lost my patience. I climb up on the railing, it's twenty meters down to the tiles of the ground floor. I balance, steadying myself with one hand on the wall while I try to catch the chain with the other. I finally reach it and pull, jumping down. The last ring of the chain gets caught on my finger, it scrapes the skin, wrenches my arm, I'm standing on tiptoe, thinking my finger's going to break, but now the hatch is wide open. The bird sits in a corner and doesn't move. I kick at it in an attempt to rouse it but it just cowers, so I yell: beat it already! I don't know how long I can keep holding the chain. Finally it flies up sluggishly, as if still undecided. It probably belongs to someone, what else would it be doing here in the cold. I can't straighten my finger to let go of the chain, it's stuck on the second-to-last joint. Finally it slides off, taking the skin with it. The finger bleeds. I see that the bird has found its way, the red feathers gleam against the gray sky, my heroic Tristan of Masada, the hatch falls shut. I press my bleeding finger into my fist and go down. Beneath me a door opens, slightly, the peephole in another door clicks, they should have opened their doors earlier, when I needed the ladder, the assholes! Now all I need is for one of them to ask if I've seen their bird!

I slam the door behind me so that the whole building shakes—I've been too quiet here!

I hold my finger under cold water, the tap full on, but as soon as I turn it off, the pain makes me furious. I fan it with a feather from the bird, maybe it was only a pet shop breed and tomorrow it will be sitting on the roof again, wanting its usual dish of seeds. Tristan!—I always get caught by words.

Masada—between Sodom and Jericho, Qumran in the North, on the Dead Sea. Every name a knock at the manor gate. It wasn't the Essenes who wrote the scrolls; history is being rewritten—new excavations, new discoveries, in Jerusalem too; the piled up layers of epochs and ages—how many times was the city destroyed?

It's only a misunderstanding that I wasn't born a Jew.

I think of the besieged: Troy, La Rochelle, Musa Dagh. I hear Mahler's "Resurrection" symphony played at Masada. I imagine a ballet on this plateau of weather-grayed whitish-yellow stone, red robes?, birds flying overhead. I feel good. My finger's swelling, my shoulder hurts; no practice today.

## 5

*Ach, nemá se tak dlouho žít!* It's a great mistake to live so long! Oh, if you could only know how easy life is for you! You are so close to life! You see in life some meaning! Life has for you some value! Fools, how happy you all are . . . And it's due to the paltry chance that you will all die soon.

*The Makropulos Affair* by Janáček.

I sit in the theater where two hundred years ago Mozart premiered his *Don Giovanni*. The colors aren't the classic theatrical red and gold, but rather blue and silver; the ornamentation is gold, the dove-gray plush of the seats heightens the impression of silver. The curtain is blue.

How much material do you need for a theater curtain? In the private castle theaters and travelling stages, instead of the heavy fabric they had cardboard with drapery drawn on it. There are famous curtains like there are famous church windows. The National Theater has three curtains: the external iron one with chased borders, the main curtain with a decorative allegory, and a fabric curtain of red velvet. Behind them are several rows of sheer material for dividing the stage.

Before the price of theater tickets was raised drastically in the last few years, busloads of people had come from the countryside, so that everyone got a chance to visit the "little chapel on the Vltava" at least once. Their ancestors had given their savings so the Czech people could build a theater of their own.

When the iron curtain opened, a murmur passed through the rows, everyone admiring the magnificent painting; then, as the hall grew dark, the heavy velvet rustled aside and the first notes sounded.

Appropriately, the words over the stage are "Národ sobě"— "The Nation for Itself." In contrast with the classicist motto over the portal of the Estates Theater: "Patriae et Musis."

The Estates Theater is a hundred years older than the National Theater, and mostly intact in its original form. Blue, tall, narrow. Built in 1783, offering German repertoire and Italian opera; an occasional Czech farce was the exception. In 1787, Mozart brought his *Don Giovanni*. When he arrived in Prague with the commissioned work, it lacked an overture, several arias, and the finale. The score and the differences in paper—he hadn't even remembered the paper!—make it easy to determine exactly which parts were written at the last minute; the music is unaffected. Praguers love *their* Mozart—in the euphoric atmosphere of universal enthusiasm and admiration he could improvise without inhibition, even throwing in allusions to members of the ensemble during the premiere, which did not escape the audience. He could have spared himself the local color: the Praguers had already accepted him.

I imagine Mozart in overdrive, hopping between piano and desk, scratching on the hastily-obtained paper—*everything's already composed, though I admit I've not yet written a note!*—a few somersaults now and then, meows, giggles (if even half of the accounts are true!), sleeves rolled up—a dainty lumberjack, for all his agitation keeping the big picture in view: *they think because I'm so small and young, there can't be anything great and old in me; but they'll soon see for themselves.*

There had already been two adaptations of the same material by Italian composers, which were known in Prague. As in the days of Michelangelo, when the citizens of Florence inspected the new artworks in the forum—the David, the Hercules, the Perseus, the Neptune fountain in front of the Palazzo Vecchio (*Ammanato, Ammanato, che bel marmo hai rovinato!*—Ammanato, what beautiful marble you've ruined!)—the Praguers could compare and judge the musical achievements of their contemporaries. Unlike in Vienna, here Mozart had to explain nothing.

A hundred years later, it was the same for Janáček, only this time Prague was the capital that wanted nothing to do with him, and Brno the provincial town where he was understood and loved.

I sit in this Mozartian opera house and hear the music of a Moravian who's performed better in Brno, and when in Prague, then in the National Theater, like the other Czech operas, instead of in this fine, cosmopolitan house filled solely with Japanese, Germans, French, Italians, and Americans.

After the war the building was renamed the Tyl Theater, after Josef Kajetán Tyl, in whose farce *Fidlovačka* the national anthem "Where My Home Is" was heard for the first time, tellingly, as the song of a blind violinist.

Since 1989, it's been the Estates Theater again. The re-renaming continues.

*The Makropulos Affair* was moved to the Estates Theater because the National Theater, after years of restoration, is closed again *z technických důvodů*, "for technical reasons"— this explanation has dogged me since childhood. For technical reasons there's been no water, no milk, no bread, no light, no trains, no cinema, no theater; the cardboard sign hung on doors where you wouldn't imagine there to be much technical in the first place: on garages, depots, wastepaper collections, libraries. The closed cinemas were the most painful. More often the message was just *back soon*.

The Janáček matinee isn't sold out, unlike the *Don Giovanni*, with the doughily sensual Ukrainian who's sung the title role every afternoon and evening without a break for three years: tall, pressing the women to his bare chest. The production doesn't lack a certain authenticity, also in the vocal suggestions of Don Ottavio's impotence and Donna Anna's hysteria; only Donna Elvira's complexity is distorted into broad comedy. Most incisive of all is the interaction between Leporello and Don Giovanni. At some point the singers have learned how to move.

*The Makropulos Affair.*

A huge clock stands on the stage, upon which a drummer dressed as a skeleton chimes the hour. *Vulnerant omnes, ultima necat.* A light goes on in the background: shelves full of files, dusty fascicles—a lawyer's office. Then a telephone call.

Čapek had discouraged Janáček, he found his own play too unpoetic—a comedy of manners, unsuited for a musical adaptation.

Janáček saw the tragedy of the main character and the dramatic potential of the material. He used the dialogue, cut the polemical ending, and condensed the confession of Emilia Marty/Elina Makropulos into a cathartic finale.

After a lifetime away, the three-hundred-year-old singer returns to Prague to find the recipe for the elixir of life, which her father had prepared for Rudolf II and tested on his daughter at the emperor's behest. She senses that she has begun to age.

She captivates everyone but remains indifferent; one man even kills himself for the love of her. When Gregor, her great-grandson, threatens to kill her if she won't love him, she shows him a scar on her neck. "Another said he'd kill me, and if I stripped myself naked in front of you then you could see all my other souvenirs! Why is it men feel that they must kill me?" She falls asleep and snores while he declares his love, she drinks and curses the chamber maid for pulling her hair when she receives the news that young Janek has killed himself for her, makes nasty jokes.

"For a long time past now I've not been a lady. Who knows how many bastards I have got roaming around the world?"

Near the end, harassed by all and cursed as a scoundrel, a thief, and a fraud, she feels close to death. You are all here now, and it's as if you were not here, you're mere shadows and dead things! Oh, if you could only know how easy life is for you! You believe in mankind, love, virtue, progress. But in me life has come to a standstill, I cannot go on. How dreadful this loneliness! There's no joy in goodness, there is no joy in evil. Joyless the earth, joyless the sky! When you know that then your soul dies within you.

Čapek had written a "comedy;" from the same material Janáček created one of the great tragic female figures. Her closing aria is reminiscent of Isolde. Both fulfill their fate; both drank something that changed their lives. Isolde had wanted to die; Elina Makropulos was just an obedient daughter. After a week of unconsciousness and convulsions, she awoke from her father's experiment and was immortal. Try it out on your daughter, the emperor had ordered! She was sixteen.

For three hundred years she's roamed the world, the daughter of the physician Hieronymus Makropulos, ιατρός Καίσαρος Ροδόλφου, as Ellian MacGregor, Elsa Miller, Ekaterina Myškina, Eugenia Montez, Emilia Marty. She switches countries, languages, and names, always keeping her initials—E. M.—and her profession: singer. By the end, as Emilia Marty, she's 337 years old.

There are several reasons I feel close to her.

Alive for three hundred years, exhausted. For the man, a night with her is full of horror and dismay. Cold as a corpse, he says. She finds the recipe, but doesn't take another dose of the elixir that runs through her veins, she's had enough.

The music sounds as if the drama was made for the opera. Though the backdrops are extremely undramatic: file folders, stage door, a hotel room.

Trial records are pored over, inheritance laws explained, information is exchanged by telephone; the cast of characters includes a clerk, a lawyer, a cleaning lady, a technician. *Sprechgesang, parlando, recitative.* And in the middle of it all, the strain on Marty from her secret, her impatience. Her presence irritates. She draws the energy of those around her and incites crimes without even noticing.

Janáček's second-to-last opera, the only one to dispense with folklore, relinquishing his infatuation with Moravia: rough, *non cantabile.*

The heavy, raging prelude, the staccato of the basses punctuated by breathless, shrill whistles, Rudolfinian fanfares, then a landscape motif, so sweet and warm it makes your heart ache. Makropulos was Greek; the sounds are Moravian. Memories of a happy childhood, with her dreams, trustfulness, curiosity towards life. The finale: farewell, acceptance of human destiny, of death. No more rushing.

No aria, no duet. My characters too are alone, they dance for themselves.

I leave in a daze, perhaps the only one in the audience who knows the opera so well that it upsets me: the story of a three-hundred-year-old woman who can't die, just slowly ages, like the Cumaean Sibyl . . . *and when the boys asked her, "Sibyl, what do you want? She answered "I want to die."* There's no other composer who can bring together dissonance at the margins of tonality with this kind of melody, this passion. At the Vienna Volksoper the conductor explained the development in the foyer before the performance; seventy years after its debut, it was still too difficult.

Janáček himself was over seventy when he finished *The Makropulos Affair.* His immortality was already assured.

**6.**

Outside it's snowing, and I wonder whether snow at least gave Makropulos pleasure—even for a three-hundred-year-old Greek, it's no everyday event. Now she'd be seventy years older, four hundred and seven. And there's less and less snow.

I hear my name. No one here would say Leonora Marty—no one who knows me from back then.

The man must be younger than me, he's standing at the side entrance to the theater next to the Mozart plaque. "Did you recognize yourself?"

He has some nerve. He'd stared at me during intermission in the cafe, nodded behind his glass, *Leporello Mix* and *Don Giovanni Cocktail*—the one a noxious green, the other a syrupy red with a sugared rim and a slice of lemon—and that at a Janáček opera. Apparently he was drinking both; he grinned. He does the same now. The two elegant Japanese women from the diplomatic corps come out giggling; why don't Japanese women ever laugh loudly? A car drives up, though this is a pedestrian zone, and they climb in as if it's a matter of course.

I remember now that he was also standing at the cloakroom when I wrestled my coat away from the crowd—I can be quick about putting it on, just to get out of the crush at all costs, out of the fatal mixture of perfume and perspiration, the pretentious chatter of the audience.

"I saw you in the piece twice." He has a slight accent—soft, the long vowels shorter—almost like a Moravian, compared to the elongated Czech of the Praguers.

"Are you from Germany?"

"I've lived in Prague for half a year."

"Ok then, goodbye." Now, in addition to the thirty thousand Americans, Germans are settling here too, and in the middle of a housing shortage. I'm also not prepared for someone from Germany to recognize me here.

He's not bothered by my manner. "Where was it? The first time was in Kassel, then in France."

"In Aix?"—he does speak Czech, at least.

"No, in Strasbourg." As if to underscore his winner, he throws a snowball at a street sign, really putting his arm into it; the "no-parking zone" rattles, slightly dented.

"Handball players are butchers," I say. I'd heard the sentence somewhere.

"Water polo," he corrects me. "By the way, I saw you in Podolí too. Do you swim often?"

He's starting to creep me out. "Are you sure?"

"I recognize your legs. This is the first time I've seen you fully dressed."

I'd deport him if I could. "Isn't this one coincidence too many?"

"They're not coincidences, I went to Strasbourg on purpose."

"Are you interested in ballet?"

"Not in the least." He looks at me. "It's just that I'm part of an institution . . ."

I walk away. I didn't come to Prague to have conversations with foreigners. I'm curious about my "compatriots," who want nothing to do with me. He keeps walking beside me, as if everything were fine.

There's a Christmas market on Old Town Square. Stalls with sausages, beer, grog, cotton candy, popcorn, pizza, crepes. The names wash over me, none of it tastes any better here.

I see a stand with potato pancakes, *bramboráky*. I try one. They're from a mix, bland, they stick to the roof of my mouth. They used to be made of shredded fresh potatoes, with onions, marjoram, and caraway. The mulled wine is sour.

He forces a Becherovka on me—it calms the stomach, he says. I'd almost forgotten why I never drink it. He eats with gusto: *klobasa* with mustard and bread, washed down with a beer; he asks if I want cotton candy or popcorn, buys toasted almonds and a baked apple on a stick, drinks an "Altvater" liqueur, seems in a great mood, while I'm growing ever testier and more impatient.

He tries to distract me with Janáček. "Czech should be the fourth language of music," he opines, "at least in this century, in the opera."

"What are the others?" I ask.

"Italian, German, French."

"Why only in fourth place?"

"Yes, I know your feelings on Janáček," he says. "I've read interviews. When you consider the fact that he was a contemporary of Puccini, and *The Makropulos Affair* was written ten years before *Lulu*. It's just that hardly anyone is aware of his modernity. In opera he's probably the greatest of the century."

"You came prepared."

"I studied the history of music and theater." He bows. "And imagine—it's probably the first Czech opera where people make telephone calls!"

I have to laugh. He's pretty funny, for a German.

Our surroundings, on the other hand, provide much less scope for mirth. Too loud, too cold, too many people. Coins are stamped, Prague groschens—coveted throughout Europe under Charles IV. Next to a glowing kettle, a man performs a love scene between a woman and a man who are drawn on his bare legs: they stretch toward one another, kiss, their mouths distend and shrink, their eyes flutter and close in the creases of his knees. It looks strangely obscene, like watching something private, and he's accordingly rewarded by the audience. His hat is full, tourists giving bills while the locals toss in coins. Elsewhere there are puppets, a twitchy fiddler keeps pace with frantic music from a boom box, bends his limbs, hovers. Colorful ribbons are braided into hair, portraits drawn, in spite of the cold and lack of light. Mimes, acrobats, magicians—the once sober populace has turned overnight into a nation of jesters, medieval jokers. Aging performance artists with red-and-green painted faces and rings in their ears display gilt garden gnomes and statesmen, which no longer shock anyone; next to them are the "new angry ones" with safety pins in their eyebrows and "the stubborn ones," who've made an installation out of a pile of cobblestones surrounded by candles and given it the title "Resistance." A group of young people sings, alternating between Christmas carols and protest songs—a reminder of the "Velvet Revolution"—and the audience is moved, they clap and sing along.

The biggest attraction for the tourists is a gypsy band with colorfully-clad dancers. They look different than the girls who stand in the arcades near Wenceslas Square under the watchful eyes of their pimps, who only turned up after the Wall fell.

I think of the young Inuits in East Greenland who danced with this same certainty to music from a crackling loudspeaker, surrounded by trash—no dirt to bury it with—in their makeshift shack-disco in Sermiligaaq: no decoration, no folklore, no superfluous gestures. Like Kleist's bear: without elegance, but it was real.

Women from Slovakia have set out their wares in the arcades near the square: Christmas decorations, like the painted eggs, plaited willow whips, and wooden rattles at Easter. They sit there in their wide skirts, wrapped up in fringed scarves of black wool, warming themselves with tea from thermoses. In the meagre light they weave little stars to hang up, and Christmas tree garlands from straw, they carve wooden figurines, animals for the crèche, they're hardly noticed amid the loud throng.

From an old woman—I once wished for a such a grandmother—I buy a straw bell and hang it on my coat button. I don't look like the kind of person who has a Christmas tree at home. Wait, girlie, she says, here's something for the cold. She reaches behind her, takes out a bottle, and pours some for me. Here's to courage and lots of children!

I almost choke on it, but my companion has the presence of mind to thump me on the back, and drinks the rest as if it's the obvious thing to do, then asks if one can buy a bottle. Auntie Hroznová'll have some, the granny says, and calls over a young farm woman who has not only homemade schnapps but also cheese: smoked and braided. It's salty but I like the consistency. I buy a braid and a pair of lambskin mittens from her neighbor—mine are falling apart—and the man buys a pair of embroidered suede slippers. You have to come to Slovakia, the beautiful old woman says, you'd like it. I know, I say, I was in Levoča as a child. There were bees.

We leave. The bazaar atmosphere continues into the side streets, the businesses are open. It's mostly exchange offices and souvenir shops: glass, porcelain, plastic—gigantic gnomes and synthetic stuffed animals peddled on the street by the Vietnamese next to the Soviet junk sold by the Russians, Ukrainians, and Kazakhs. The guesthouses near the square are filled with blustering tourists trying to be merry at all costs. The clock strikes seven. The apostles go around, the cock crows, Death pulls the cord. *Ultima necat.*

My head spins. The Slivovitz would never be allowed in a store: too pure, too strong; it smells of plums, but not only of plums. The man hardly bothers me anymore, especially since he can no longer walk straight and is finally keeping his mouth shut. The bottle is rapidly emptying.

We reach Palach Square. For twenty years after the war it was called the Square of Red Army Soldiers, in honor of the fallen Soviet soldiers who were deployed here on May 9, 1945 against the retreating Germans. In January 1969 it was briefly, spontaneously renamed Jan Palach Square, before it relapsed to the earlier name for another twenty years. Now the name Jan Palach is official, without risk, without tension or any pressure to remember—this task has been taken over by the signs. There's no collective memory in the long term, only collective forgetting.

On the quay behind the Rudolfinum a band is playing: an old couple, the man plays violin, the woman sings—guttural Russian female vocals. A young man, perhaps their son, plays balalaika. The circle of listeners is small. It's strange that they've chosen here to play and sing in Russian: the spot is hard to get to because of construction on Mánes Bridge. As if they don't want any more attention and are really playing for themselves. They're singing Jewish songs: *что растет без корня, что горит без пламени* . . . then the song of the calf brought to market. The boy puts away the balalaika and starts to dance—we always fall for their folklore—then he jumps onto the railing, does a handstand, and people clap, sing along; the coins fly.

A dancer from our troupe, a Pole, bungee-jumped from a 60-meter-high crane on the Place Stansilas, in Nancy. Naked to the waist, his skin pale, his ribs protruding, as if crucified. He'd swung over the square several times, unfolding a Polish and a French flag, stitched together, that he'd pulled from his pants pocket in memory of the Polish king and Duke of Lorraine, Stanisław Leszczyński. His Tunisian friend, wearing a tight tricot with *Vive la Pologne! Vive la France!*, walked around the monument to the duke with a hat collecting money from the impressed and confused citizens of Nancy. Both later left the ensemble; maybe bungee jumping was more fun.

The young Russian jumps down from the railing, without a flag—I'm happy to give money just for that—he bows, the family moves on and the audience too, dispersing cheerfully. I clap and dance for myself, *Dona dona dona doonaj!*, my companion stands on his hands and looks a little like a bear: a private performance for me. "Now the railing!" I laugh.

And he really does hoist himself up there, takes a few "steps"; the railing bends where the steps lead down to the river. "That's not all!" he cries with his head facing downward, and takes the curve. Well-practiced, he springs onto the steps; his hair hangs down, it looks funny. I'm starting to get used to him; up to now I've rarely been cheerful here.

Except now he's disappeared.

I lean over the railing. The streetlamps above me are blinding, I can't see anything below. I go to the steps and stare into the darkness. "Hello, where are you?" I don't even know his name. I think I can hear something below. I want to go down, but I slip and whoosh down the stairs at some speed. I prepare myself for a hard crash, but instead I'm suddenly in the water, I feel it in my nose, so icy it hurts. I automatically try to swim but my heavy clothes pull me down. I search for the bottom with my feet and as I'm finally able to stand up, something moves next to me. "Welcome to the Vltava," he says.

I look at him. "What's your name, actually?"

"I thought you knew me."

"What?"

He laughs, or at least that's what I understand through his jittering. "Let me give you my card . . ." he pats down his dripping coat. "Asperger. Thomas Asperger. I suppose you'd say Tomáš."

"I suppose I'd say Asperger, if anything! Anyway, this is all your fault!"

"Why my fault? Who said 'go on the railing'?"

"I didn't say 'go on the railing.' I said 'now the railing.'"

"It's the same thing."

"How could I know that you'd really do it? And I didn't say you should take the curve!"

"I wanted to jump down at the stairs, but it was pretty slippery." He looks up.

We traipse out of the pit.

"And what's water doing here anyway?" I look around. "Why is there a hole? There are supposed to be cobblestones here!"

"Well, I'm not sure if that would really have been better." He hobbles over a pile of frozen gravel.

The construction pit is clearly signed, the cordons are even lit up. "A little late," he mumbles.

We can see everything clearly now. One can get used to the darkness, especially since the streetlights are reflected in the river. The steps are iced over, a smooth slanted plane, we won't make it up that way. When did I last swim in the Vltava? I see ice at the edge where we didn't break through. And when did I last go ice skating on the Vltava?

We look for the next set of steps. One is boarded up, another closed off with a chain, it's not been salted either, but a path has been trod down in the middle. "Access at your own risk."

It's arduous to climb the steep stairs in our wet clothes, the water trickles off us but has almost stopped by the time we reach the top. Instead, our pant legs are forming a crust.

We wave like crazy for taxis but the only ones passing are full, none stops. We talk over each other, switching languages, a mixture of German and Czech, he wants to stick to Czech but I get impatient and shout in German—it's quicker.

He remembers that he'd left his bag and walks the three hundred meters back to the first steps. We drink the rest of the Slivovitz. "Here are your mittens," he says. "And I could put on the slippers. Actually we've got it pretty cozy. When I think that you wanted to rescue me . . ."

I hear my teeth chattering and am suddenly furious. His jokes are getting on my nerves. He ought to get lost already, leave me alone, leave the city even and take all the others with him. The East Germans above all, who've become megalomaniacs with their new Western currency and think they can do whatever they want here! They dump their broken refrigerators and trash across the border; before, they'd done it at home but now they come here with their rubbish. The woods along the border are full of their junk!

"But there aren't any woods there," he says. "Up north ..."

"I know what it's like up north!" I run over the bridge, enraged that still no cars will stop. He follows.

"Keep shouting," he says, "it'll warm us up."

I compose myself somewhat and look at him. "What's your name again?"

"Again, my name is Asperger."

With great effort, I grin. "Well then, Asperger, find us some transportation!"

He runs to the telephone booth on the corner; it's broken. A car with boisterous Americans honks at us, they're hanging out the windows with their baseball caps waving a flag, but they don't stop.

"If you're going to make so much noise around here, you should at least be good for something and stop for us!"

"You'd prefer to kick them all out, am I right? The Germans, the Americans."

"Right!"

"The Czechs too?"

"With their Velvet Revolution and all their kitsch!"

"You're a racist," he shakes his head. "But here we are talking and meanwhile we're freezing our asses off."

"What?"

"Excuse me, we're *chatting,* of course."

My face is so stiff that I can't even grimace. I start to cough but the cough turns into an attack of shivering that won't stop. I lean on the balustrade, my knees threaten to give out under me.

"Don't give in now! Stay on your feet!" He runs into the road and stumbles in front of a taxi that's barreling past.

"Fucking idiot!" the driver roars, horrified and clearly relieved that nothing happened. "I'm booked!"

"Here!" Asperger waves a wet hundred-mark bill under his nose and stuffs me into the car. The driver sees our dripping clothes and starts to say something, but Asperger gives him a look that suggests he'll attack him if he doesn't start driving.

I manage to get out the address through chattering teeth and then I'm pretty much out of it. I see my right foot hitting the floor, rhythmically, loudly, I can't make it stop. A puddle is forming next to the foot, it joins with a puddle coming from Asperger. The seat underneath us is soaked. Asperger holds me tight, I feel him shivering, he's having trouble talking too.

I'm ten years old, I've just fallen into the water at Stromovka, the Royal Game Reserve—the pond only had a skim of ice covered with a dusting of snow. My father, a Communist, pulls me up the hill, tries to keep me on my feet. A car with an open door is waiting in front of the Soviet Embassy, the driver is leafing through a newspaper. "Comrade, my little girl just fell through the ice, I have to get her into bed immediately!" The driver balks—the attaché is on his way, this is his official car, he has his orders. My father actually convinced this anxious civil servant to drive us. At the gate in Dejvice he said that was fine, we'd walk through the underpass, and thanks a lot! He carried me on his back the rest of the way. The puddle I'd left in that fancy car was no smaller than our joint one now, even though my father had held me on his lap the whole time. I see the military attaché or whatever they called their KGB officers, impatient after his long wait, finally sitting down on a lace doily behind the Zim's closed curtains, and then getting out of the car with a wet behind.

That was the first time that my father revealed himself to me as a Communist. Otherwise he was inconspicuous, friendly to the point of inanity, not very practical. He took his membership seriously. We couldn't even have a piano, he gave everything away. He took the doctrine of collective ownership literally. People laughed about him; otherwise they were mostly fearful—he creeped them out.

He'd been a Communist even before the war. After his voluntary service on the barricades, like hundreds of thousands of other cheering Praguers he'd enthusiastically greeted the Soviet liberators. Over the next days, he'd taken soldiers through the streets and shown them the city. He took the children along—my elder sister was four at the time. In St. Vitus Cathedral a giant of a Russian had stepped on her foot when he was looking at the ceiling. The acoustics were appropriate; before she'd even stopped hollering the giant lifted her onto his shoulders, and he carried her through the city the whole rest of the day. She held tight to his head, was taller than everyone else, she enjoyed the view. He smelled of tobacco and machine oil, a tankist. He had two little girls at home, Sascha and Vera. And what was her name? Marie. Ah, Marusja. Maschenka, *пра́вильно*, very pretty. He rocked her on the dizzying heights of his shoulders, singing unintelligibly but somehow familiarly, and she shrieked and clung to his hair. Her hero. The end of the war was one big festival of tall, good-smelling men. In comparison, the women at home were taciturn, emaciated, rarely sang, dressed in men's duds they fetched water, fixed what was broken, provided for daily life, and they didn't smell nearly as nice and Christmassy as before.

After the war my father managed a large textile business in Carlsbad; the downturn came later, in Prague, when he was made the deputy of a younger, teetotalling director: he sold carpets and linoleum in the basement, usually he carried the heavy rolls without help, never complained, died alone.

During the war when my sister was little, he took her with him to fetch coal; when she couldn't walk anymore he put her in the sack and talked to her the whole way. People stared, perplexed to see him talking to a sack. On payday in Carlsbad he usually came home with a chain of sausages around his neck, and we kids hung off him and ate them from the chain. The cats waited for us to throw them the casings, and my mother berated him—this is how you separate yourself from people! Look at you, you look like a *šupák*! Your last suit!—and then she'd start laughing.

The memory makes me warm.

We get out and a chill shoots through me again, I can't get the key out of my coat pocket, can't get it into the lock; finally Asperger manages to unlock the door. We have to wait for the elevator, we wouldn't make it to the fifth floor with our stiff knees. We have the same problem with the apartment door; he's in as bad shape as I am—I've rarely seen lips so blue. He looks at mine, probably thinking the same thing.

It's hardly warmer in the apartment than on the street. He orients himself immediately, plugs in the radiator, turns the heating knob, but to no avail. Then he sees the poster on the wall. "No offense to your compatriots, but doesn't the *important artist* in their city deserve something better than this freezing dump?"

I shake my head. "Firstly, my compatriots are often worse off. And you know nothing about the "important artist." And finally, leave my compatriots out of it!" My shivering hasn't stopped.

I take off my things—the wet boots can only be peeled off with difficulty—clumsily get into the bathtub, and turn on the shower. I don't want to take long, he's waiting too, but I don't get warm, especially since half of the weak stream of water squirts out to the side: the showerhead isn't sealed.

I only grow a little less stiff. I open the shower curtain: he's standing in front of the tub, naked, shivering. I leave the water on. I wrap myself in a bath towel and go into the room, looking for dry clothes—for him as well. In the wardrobe that's been left there are a few shirts, sweaters, socks, a tracksuit. I lay everything on the bed and try to make tea. Drawing water and putting the plug of the immersion heater into the socket takes effort, everything is slowed by the fact that I'm wracked by chills and can hardly hold the things; pulling out the plug is as difficult as putting it in. When I finally pour the boiling water through the strainer, I'm exhausted and impressed by my own achievement. Asperger gets out of the tub: a door was supposed to be installed between the kitchen and bathroom ages ago, but I never see the landlord to remind him. "There's stuff to wear in the room." I hand him a dry towel.

He doesn't seem to have warmed up either. When I bring the tea, he's just putting on his lambskin slippers. "Perfect timing!" he shivers, pleased.

I pour him a cup.

"Do you have rum? Milk or sugar, at least? Don't tell me there's nothing to warm us up, in this cold!" He stands up and looks in the kitchen cabinet, which I rarely open, full of spilled spices in decaying paper bags, aroma-less coffee and hardened salt in open containers, the remains of the landlord's abandoned household. "We've got everything!" He brings over a dusty, labelless bottle and a sticky sugar bowl with a few yellowed sugar cubes, blows away some dead ants along with the sugar dust—"I have these little red ones too!" He seems pleased at the reunion, or at our similarity—and sniffs at the bottle. "It doesn't look like rum. It's something bitter. Fernet! Some for you?"

"No," I climb fully dressed into bed and lean against the wall. "There are blankets," I point to the wardrobe.

"We can make music, dance, move our bodies!" he says.

I look up and can't quite recognize him, he looks mis-shapen—either from the worn-out track suit or from my blurred vision. My eyes burn. I lie down, huddle under the duvet, but the shivering still doesn't stop.

"Wait." He comes over, rubs my back, my arms, my legs, my neck; the movement warms him up.

I can't speak. I turn on my side, continue shivering.

"Just don't get sick," he bends over me. "I love you, you see."

I duck under the covers, waiting for the waves of shivering to stop, but instead they get worse and alternate with waves of heat.

"But I'm sure you've long-since figured that out."

"Hm," I say, in order not to appear surprised, and curl up into a ball. I just want to sleep.


My mother stands on the street with my father's suit over her arm, dry-cleaning tags hang from the sleeve and pants, the legs nearly reach the ground. Look at you. So gloomy. So unfeminine. Other girls are like sparks. At your age, they already have responsibilities, and you just read.

They have children.

She suppresses a laugh. In that case, better stick with books! And don't be so late home from the cinema. Here are ten crowns.

My father shakes his head. And I always thought she'd end up short and fat. She can be a nurse if she makes some effort.

She's going to study, says my mother.

Don't be so gloomy!

I look into her dark, gloomy face. I'm like her, only not so pretty, and twenty centimeters taller.

Make me a little coffee, *kafíčko*, says my father. She'll be a nurse, short and chubby. The lisp is charming, let them laugh, they're dumb.

A nurse. *Kafíčko.*

Don't be so gloomy. Get some fresh air, meet people!

Short and chubby.

Nurse.

Smile.

*Kafíčko.*

That's why he died alone.

I was already gone. She was dead, and I went out to meet people.


I open my eyes.

Drying banknotes hang on the line above me: Czechoslovakian hundreds, including a Gottwald, issued a few months before the administration stepped down, the most hideous and most pointless form of currency, shrunken, the bilious green color faded and smudged. The brown tens might be even uglier, but they're smaller. The German bills keep their color; the watermark and silver thread are easy to make out against the light. Gauss with a kind of nightcap, apparently toothless, Clara Schumann dumbed down into Biedermeier harmlessness, the Brothers Grimm frozen in a strange brownish violet; the old engravings were nicer. The Austrian physics Nobel Prize-winner Schroedinger looks pinched and crumpled, Mozart's nose is too long; the water had no power over the hologram on the new five thousand crown note. Freud looks down in distress from a grimy fifty.

I'm thirsty.


The man comes closer. He stands over me, in a thick sweater with a scarf around his neck; he looks more domestic here than I ever have. "Money laundering," he points to the bills. "The ones on the left are yours. Are you often in Austria?"

I shake my head, I don't want to speak, I'm not sure I can. I swallow carefully; a pain I've known since childhood shoots through me. An abscess, I need antibiotics. Unfortunately hardly anything works on me anymore. The tetracycline I was given after the weeks I was forced to spend with my classmates in a work brigade during the hops harvest ruined the efficacy of just about everything else. I'm resistant, just not against tonsillitis.

He looks at me pensively, with concern. Tries to smile when I look at him. I can't exactly remember why he's here or what he wants.

Apparently he knows my face pretty well.

"Asperger," he says. "It's still Asperger. Remember? My God, is it so hard? Then just call me Tomáš already!"

I try to grin. My face is no longer so stiff, but it still hurts. I touch my throat.

"Yes, that's what I thought! I have the same scratchiness. Here are lozenges and drops. I couldn't get anything else without a prescription. I'll call a doctor."

I shake my head.

"Fine, not now. But later."

He props me up while I laboriously swallow a bitter liquid. "And now an aspirin and a sip of tea. Good girl." He kisses my forehead as if it were the most natural thing in the world and disappears into the kitchen.

I lie back down.

As if from a great distance I see him whistling, pulling tools out of the cabinet in the hallway, clattering about with the heating, turning, tightening something, blowing, jiggling, the water starts to bubble. "So, it'll soon be a lot warmer in here. I didn't want to make too much noise while you were sleeping.

How long? Two days.

Me? I'm staying here. I already called. There's a telephone in the building. Do you know Mrs. Molnárová downstairs? She knows you. She recognized you on the poster. She has a cat . . . she wanted to bring you soup.

No? Ok, I'll tell her you can't swallow."

He puts a hand on my forehead. "You should really be in the hospital. Take another aspirin! Here's some juice. And if the fever doesn't go down by evening . . . let me feel your pulse . . . What did you do to yourself?"

I flinch when he touches my finger. I shake my head. I don't want to speak. What does he know of Tristan from Masada.

"If it doesn't get better by tonight, I'm calling a doctor! I have to go now, get some other clothes and something to eat. Will you be ok alone?" Apparently he considers himself indispensable. I nod.

"Do you need anything else? Water, mineral water, yes. And juice. There are your clothes, already mostly dry," he points to a second clothesline and at the radiator. "But stay in bed. I'll be back as quick as I can."

He takes a few bills from the line and leaves.

Another landscape, another light. The sky stretches. An older man stands hunched over an evaporator, the flasks bubble and hiss, everything is shrouded in colorful smoke. It's my father; I can't make him out, he won't look at me. Where is my mother? Would she have let him go, far from the sun of Crete, to a cold, unfriendly city in the north, would she have even let him take their daughter with him? What she never would have allowed: that he try out his brew on me!

—She's always been good. Obedient. She'll do it.

—She's going to study! She has a gift for languages. She can dance!

—Try it on your daughter! the emperor had commanded.

Is there anything more ill-fated than an obedient father?

The mother wasn't there, in that narrow alley of gray stone where alchemists from all over Europe thronged, taking it in turns to sleep. The laboratories with their cauldrons, flasks, crucibles, and evaporators were beneath the castle, in the cellars and abandoned dungeons; it was a place of agitation, delirium, elemental martyrdoms in which the passion of Christ was invoked, chymical weddings of King Sulphur with Queen Mercury, Saturn with lead, the color black, melancholia, black bile. The feverish, lurching search for happiness, for gold, for the manifold elixirs of life, of eternal youth, for the philosopher's stone. Rivals by day, united at night by the vermin, the miasmas, the dampness of the bear pit under their dollhouse windows, by the view of the dungeon—a warning—by cold sweat. If, in all the misfortune, they got lucky, they might end up one day as attractions at the market fair on Old Town Square, in wooden stalls, touting ointments, deer antler glue, iron vitriol and cassia oil, like the famous Geronimo Alessandro Scotta: down and out, but alive. There were prisons, the dungeon and—hangmen, on days when the emperor's patience wore thin. Some had a more appropriate exit, like the "Most Serene Count" Mamugna from Famagusta, the great sorcerer who was hanged in a golden gown from gilt gallows and then dumped in a pauper's grave with his two Luciferian black mastiffs. And Kelley—Master Edward Kelley, doctor of both kinds of magic, the most influential favorite of the emperor—anyone who got on his bad side didn't last long. He was rumored to be able to make himself invisible. And so, one day, he disappeared.

The father came to the tower. —How was the emperor to know that his elixir worked?

The distant father: ἰατρός Καίσαρος Ροδόλφου. I did his washing, served his cronies, his mistresses. She'll be a nurse, good, obedient. He wanted ones with spirit, like her mother.—Don't be obedient, my daughter! She was already dead.—Or the cool, unapproachable ones. Brigitte Helm in *Metropolis*, the machine woman.

When Ufa newsreels were shown in Prague under the Protectorate, there was often vocal protest from the cinema patrons, against which even the official chaperones and admonishing slide projections before the show were powerless. Despite prison sentences—eight days for each arrestee—and threats to close the cinemas entirely, the antifascist campaigns and the boycott of the Ufa newsreels, which glorified the German war, persisted. Cinema owners edited out provocative sequences, occasionally even destroyed whole films. Otherwise the patrons threatened to demolish the theaters; they loudly demanded the familiar Fox and Paramount as well as their home-grown news and refused to be put off.

—To the unknown cinema patrons.

I surface and sink back down again, the countless streaks of time capture me, carry me, pull me into the sleep of a three-hundred-year-old, a notorious cinema-goer and compulsive tram-rider.

The 22 races down the open stretch between Belvedere and Prague Castle—the nicest stretch of tramline I know. Then on to Brusnice, Pohořelec, Malovanka, Marijánka, Drinopol, Under the Chestnut, White Mountain.

It doesn't stop at the site of the Baroque defeat but races on, backward into history, to the valley of Wild Šárka and the bloody climax of the mythological Maidens' War, when Vlasta, the commander, had the beautiful Šárka tied to a cliff as a decoy for the fierce Ctirad. When he tried to free her, the women ambushed him and his companions, killed them all, and brought the nobleman to their castle and displayed him, braided on the wheel, on the battlements as a warning to the other men. This so infuriated Přemysl, the widower of Libuše, since whose death the women had so dropped in esteem and respect that they preferred war to the humiliations of daily life, that he fell upon them with an army of men that far outnumbered them and quelled the uprising; none was spared. The Maiden's Castle—Děvín—was razed to the ground so that no trace was left of the erstwhile power and resistance of the women. The rebellion was banished to the realm of myth.

Three hundred or three thousand years: the valley stretches, the gray cliffs lighten, become sand, the thicket disappears, no more green, heat. The 22 races through the scorching valley of the queens: sand in the eyes, in the nose, in the hair, in the mouth; grinding teeth, salty and bitter. Then faultlines and sand dunes between it all, ossified in the lee, a break from the Aeolian processes. Below, in the depths of artesian wells, fossil water. I've traveled a long way: the cat cemetery in Bubastis, the pyramids, the sphinx, the second cat cemetery in Beni Hasan, three hundred kilometers further up the Nile. The tram rattles along, toward Abu Simbel far to the south, through Nubia, from the first cataract in Aswan to the second near Wadi Halfa, to the third just before Kerma, to the fourth, where Meroë and Napata were once Egypt's capitals, to the fifth and six cataracts in Sudan, three thousand kilometers upriver.

The heat increases. Along my way are Giza, Memphis, Karnak, Luxor, Deir el-Bahari. I'm Hatshepsut, Maatkare Hatshepsut, formed by the ram-headed god Khnum on his potter's wheel, while Thoth documented my creation in writing. Hatshepsut, at the feet of Amun-Ra, king of the gods—his especial favorite. I wear the double crown, I am the sovereign of upper and lower Egypt. My name is carved into a cliff at Aswan, next to the name of my trusted steward and supervisor Senenmut. With his help I had wood brought from the land of Nega, reopened the turquoise mines of Sinai, and restored the Temple of Hathor. My barges, laden with precious wood and blocks of granite, surely landed at Thebes.

I open new trade routes, have spices, panther skins, metals, and gems brought to my land—for the dead and for those still living, I have gilded obelisks erected and holy barques built. I send an expedition across the Red Sea into the fabled realm of Punt, land of incense, and the ships return with thirty-one frankincense trees with the topsoil still clinging to their roots, which are planted before the terrace of my temple at Deir el-Bahri. The grains of frankincense are measured in bushels and weighed against gold; there is also ebony, ivory, terebinth resin, pepper, wild animals, monkeys, and greyhounds. The only thing missing is dancing dwarves. The prince of Punt has a fat wife. I am Hatshepsut. I drink from the udder of the mother goddess Hathor. The great queen. M. for Maatkare. My funerary temple, the "holy of holies," is completed. Not all of the cartouches could be destroyed.

Maatkare, the queen. The lid of the third coffin closes over me. It echoes, the shock waves carry the distant sound down to me. The ointment-soaked bandages and cloths squeeze me tight. I can't move. I'm hollow inside, my entrails have been pulled out through the openings—through my mouth and nose. I make no sound. My eyes, whether I close them or open them—the same darkness. Noises? Blood in my ears? My heart? My heart is enclosed in an alabaster dish behind a gilded wall next to the coffin, inlaid with lapis lazuli, obsidian, sapphires, pearls, and emeralds. Garlands of flowers lie atop the coffin.

My tongue? I feel around in my empty mouth. What do I feel with? My teeth are there. I have my eyes. It's difficult to open them, the cloths are tight, my nostrils are covered, as is my mouth. It's stuffy. What do I breathe with? Do I have lungs? They've been torn out, like my stomach, liver, gallbladder, and kidneys. My brain? Removed. Through my nose. I feel no pain. I am light.

The only heavy thing is the golden mask on my face, with the royal cobra and vulture on the forehead.

Was the ritual carried out according to the highest laws? Senenmut would have seen to that. My daughter, where is my clever Neferure? Be not obedient, my daughter. Were only precious materials, stones, and metals used? Are my cats with me? Did the embalming take twelve days?

I can already hear them chiseling everything away—the portraits from the walls, the statues, my obelisks, the inscriptions, my cartouches. My nephew is in a hurry.

I tear the blanket away from my face. The heat behind my eyes and behind my forehead lingers, but breathing is easier. I drink a sip of water, then fall back, float on time's layer of air. I am a mummy, a robot, I am Leni Riefenstahl. I am every fossil, intent on perfection.

For her Olympics film, one hundred cameramen shot five hundred kilometers of material; just going through it took several weeks. For Hitler's second party congress she had a hoist built on a flagpole for the aerial shots; Hitler got his own camera, which focused only on him during his appearances, capturing his best poses. She held it in the palm of her hand, the chance to show up the spectacle for the false puppet show it was. Instead she was a co-producer, perfecting the impact of the show.

In her first takes the improvised, amateurish aspect is still visible: Hitler strides aimlessly across the lawn, returns just as pointlessly, his minders shoo away anyone who tries to come too close. She wants nothing to do with this first film, she didn't have enough material, couldn't edit, the *Sturmabteilung* had hindered the shooting. She complains to Hitler; he gives orders. The second party congress in 1934 is a great success. She wanted to make not a document, but a work of art. The waving of the flags, the undulation of the massive swathes of fabric with huge swastikas, and in contrast the sheen of polished boots in lockstep, descending stairs erected specially for the film; fire, torches, obelisks. And over and over the same lonely Führer: under the triumphal arch, on the speaker's platform, standing in an open car; from behind, in semi-profile, against the evening sun, the most flattering angle. Then the choruses of work battalions shouldering spades, the tirelessly cheering masses.

She would have filmed for Stalin too, she said. Not happily, just as she hadn't been happy to film for Hitler, but she would have filmed.

She isn't a party member. She's not interested in politics. But when the Germans march into Paris she sends Hitler an enthusiastic congratulatory telegram: Mein Führer! . . .

There's a film from the seventies that exemplifies the true nature of filmmakers: a reporter has a camera built into his eye and films his subject—a terminally ill woman in a future city populated by the young and healthy: day and night, every moment, without her knowledge—as her friend and companion. Since she's on the run from the health authorities and lives in hiding, she doesn't know that her every step, the progressive stages of her illness, her death, are being aired daily, nationwide, at prime time. The man is all eye. He can't turn the camera off. In the end he tears his eye out in shame, becomes blind.

Riefenstahl would have left the camera running.

She was tough. In her first films, before she began directing, she was a mountain climber, a pilot, a dancer. Then she discovered that her true talent lay in filmmaking, shooting, editing. Her Nazi sympathies earned her a ban on making films after the Nuremburg trials. If I were a man, nothing would have happened to me, she said.

At seventy she became certified to scuba dive, giving her age as twenty years younger. At ninety she dove and shot underwater films with a younger man whom she'd trained on the camera.

In a documentary, she sits on the bed at her summer house in a short nightgown, showing off her ninety-year-old legs—slim, smooth, tanned—critically watching her most recent takes. Next to her, her aging husband, forty years younger. Another decade and he would be too old for her.

She's the most astonishing German woman of her century. She's professional. She would have left the camera running no matter what.

I'm cold.

The man is back, trying to be quiet. I watch him, he squints over at me, and I play dead, pretending to sleep. There's no more heat, no more seething blood. The slow, monotonous flowing of thin blood through blue veins, for three hundred years.

I hear him rustling shopping bags in the kitchenette, turning on the gas stove, putting water on to boil, cracking eggs into the pan. It hisses, sizzles: bacon—he doesn't know that I only eat vegetables and fish. Should I give him a lecture on the diet of a dancer? It smells good.

I open my eyes. He's standing over me. "I know you're not sleeping anymore," he says. "When you're asleep, you grind your teeth. Nice to have you back." He touches my temples. "And the fever is gone, too! Now just tell me you're hungry."

"I'm hungry."

"She can speak!" he kisses my hand enthusiastically, he had better not make a habit of it. "Shall I bring you the food in bed?"

"No, I'm getting up!" I say testily. I feel sweaty, sticky all over. "How long did I sleep?"

"A long time. Today is the fifth day. You woke up a few times, but you weren't responsive. You were pretty far gone." He looks at me.

"What day is today?" I ask.

"I couldn't say either," he says. "Being with you is like being on an island, a quarantine island—there's no contact, no interaction with the rest of the population."

"And in the end, everyone's dead. The ship of the dead."

"Except that our ship has arrived safely in the harbor and they're letting us come ashore." He looks young, confident, and in love.

I imagine choreographing the disembarkation from the ship of the dead. The railing as backdrop, a pas de deux in front of the gangway; no, it would have to be two men and a woman. Pas de trois. *Verklärte Nacht.* And then a step dance on the shaft tunnel. *Mister Bojangles.*

If there's a first opera where people speak on the telephone, there can be a first ballet where people dance on a shaft tunnel. An ocean liner, women in airy white suits playing shuffleboard, like Greta Garbo; bathers around the swimming pool, promenading on deck. And suddenly all the deckchairs are tilted, the wine glasses slide off the tables, water squeezes through the portholes; a dance on an inclined plane. And then the rescue at the quay of the Vltava.

The icy cobblestones in front of the landing stage; the lamps from the street; gulls on wires above the dancers; the carriages from Old Town Square with the tipsy drivers in their greasy bowlers; the gypsy band come to greet the survivors; the taxis rushing by without stopping, full of happy Americans who don't shrink from waving their flag here, in my Prague. Is it even my Prague still? It lacks a fountain, bubbling, even in the summer it's missing from the square; I need cataclysms for my finale, and a saxophone, like in Ravel; trumpets, Janáček's trumpets, and kettledrums.

As if my stories didn't have happy endings.


I get up, throw back the blanket and freeze: there's a huge bloodstain on the sheet, dried at the edges, the same thing on my pajama pants. Asberger whistles cheerfully in the kitchen and I feverishly consider whether I have any supplies—cotton wadding, at least. As always, the blood has come unexpectedly and too early, too strong, a loss of blood that can't be quickly compensated; but still better than the panic the time it didn't come. While I'm here playing dead, three hundred years or three thousand, hollow inside, my body doesn't give a damn and continues on as it pleases.

I pull up the sheet, put on a long sweater over my pajamas and walk to the bathroom, clumsily, the skin on my legs taut. I suck in my stomach and tense my muscles, trying not to let any blood drip onto the floor. Asperger leaves the kitchen so that I can undress in the bathroom. This apartment has some serious disadvantages.

I look in the mirror. My eyes are red and my face softened, puffy from lying so long in the heat. A cramp worms through my abdomen, a familiar pain. Isn't there any more reliable way of assuring oneself of one's continued existence?

I take a long, laborious shower, enjoying the soapsuds on my skin, the shampoo, the warmth, the water splashing on my hair, my mouth, my closed eyes. The water pressure seems stronger than before. Then a cold rinse; I suppress my usual shriek, rub myself down. The towel is streaked with blood, I put it in a bucket to soak with the pajama pants and look for cotton. There's a tiny bit, it won't last half an hour. I dress and look in the hallway; there's exactly one tampon left in the pack. Asperger is waiting for me, and the food is long-since cold. "I didn't know you liked showering *that* much." He smiles, disappointed, and takes the plates back into the kitchen, turns on the stove. While it sizzles in the pan he rinses the plates again. "Otherwise it won't look so good," he says.

In that moment, I like him.

"Would you like a soup first?" he asks. "There's tomato soup and broccoli soup." He shows me the cans.

"Maybe tomato soup, later," I say. I don't want to disappoint him again.

We eat his fried eggs, I haven't eaten bacon in years; I praise everything and he says it's too dry because it had to go back in the pan. He takes away the plates and brings cheese, red wine. He asks if I'd like coffee and cake afterwards.

My mouth begins to twitch at the sight of the red wine. "No, thank you, just a piece of cheese, I have to go out in a sec and get something."

"You can't think that I'll let you go out, with your wet hair and your cold! I can get it for you. What do you need?"

"I want to buy it myself!" I say, agitated.

"You're not leaving the apartment! It's at least ten degrees below, and you're just over pneumonia. Not quite over!"

"How do you know? Besides, if you weren't here, I'd just go."

"But I am here!"

"And I'd like to know why!"

"So that I can get you what you need, for instance! If I'm not allowed to call a doctor. That was already unwise, and risky! I thought . . ."

"What?"

"Nothing. It looked bad on the third day. I was imagining    "

"What were you imagining?"

"Nothing! Anyway, I'm not letting you go out!"

"You were imagining I was dead," I say. "What would you have done?"

"I don't know! Stupid question!" He looks at me. "What do you need?"

"I need . . . soap."

"What?"

"And cotton wadding."

"Is that all?"

"Yes, two packs."

"And you're making this fuss just for that!" He takes his coat and slams the door behind him.

I take off the sheet and scrub it in the bathroom with the towel and pajama pants. My raw fingers make it difficult, and a bluish pink spot remains on the fabric that I can't get out either with lemon or salt; I squeeze water through the sheet one more time and lay it over the radiator, I take the mattress and scrub the pad. My fingers grow stiff under the cold water, but not as bad as five days ago when I couldn't hold the key and Asperger had to unlock the door. I lean the mattress against the heater, which is now working again, and he fixed the shower too. What's his first name? — Thomas, Tomáš.

I put his three mattresses together under the window and the bedclothes in the wardrobe; that's the best I can do for domesticity in this small space. I do a few exercises, but the stomach pains keep me from doing much, and I turn on the radio. The water levels of the Bohemian waterways at seven this morning, then the weather forecast—the world exists again.

Asperger opens the door, snowy, and brings in the fresh, cold air. The snow melts on his eyelashes, he shakes off his coat, his hair, and hands me a full shopping bag. "I hope that's the right one."

I take out the soap and two packs of cotton wadding. Underneath there's a big pack of Tampax. I look at him.

"I saw an empty box in the garbage can, *regular*, is that right?"

"Yes, half of this would have been enough," I mumble.

"Well, I don't know," he glances at the drying sheet and the mattress. "I thought it couldn't hurt."

"What is this?" I take a brown jar out of a smaller bag.

"Magnesium. I went to the pharmacy too. You look so pale and drained of blood, I thought it wouldn't be a bad idea."

"Hm, thanks," I say, putting everything away. "By the way, it's not ten degrees outside, only just above freezing!"

"And at the peaks of the Ore Mountains?" he asks.

I have to laugh.

## 7.

Over the next days he puts up a curtain between the kitchen and bathroom to replace the missing door, using a drill that he's rustled up somewhere, and making a fair amount of noise. I hear the word "dowel" for the first time. The kitchen cupboard contains two new pots and a cast-iron pan; I'd found even the dishes that were already there superfluous. By now he's gotten to know all the shops in the neighborhood and a third of the residents of the building; a few of them have already started greeting him.

At first he suggested I move into his apartment, which would have been larger, warmer, more comfortable, but now he likes it here, above all the tram line to Břevnov, he doesn't even have to transfer—the 22 goes to Vinohrady, where he lives.

"Don't you know that Praguers don't like to switch sides of the river, if they ever move house? It happens rarely enough anyway."

He cooks every day; it's mostly calorie-rich, "good Bohemian food": exactly the kind of cooking I could never tolerate. It tastes astonishingly good. I put on weight and feel well.

"And where are my *frutti di mare*?"

"Yes, Highness, but we're in Bohemia; I know to your people Bohemia is on the coast, but the fishing industry doesn't entirely agree. And the calamari would prefer it a bit warmer. And perhaps with more water." It's almost Christmas.

We have different ideas about how it's to be celebrated. There's carp for Christmas, I say. And goose for New Year's.

Precisely the other way around, he contends.

Since suddenly everything in the apartment works—the light switches, appliances, and light bulbs are all intact, there are fresh flowers and unprecedented stores of potatoes, vegetables, oil, and spices—it's starting to feel too domestic for me, too cozy, too cramped. High time for him to leave. He counters my moods and special requests with calm assurance. I try to get him on thin ice.

"How about some German food?"

"Swabian dumplings? Or the national dish, fried potatoes?" he asks zealously.

I pull a face.

"Or better, Pichelsteiner stew."

"Gaah!"

"How about lentils?"

"The Germans don't know how to make lentils," I say. "Too thick, too fatty; a brown, undefined mush. Czech lentils are green, thin, sour, each lentil an individual."

"Even in the kitchen you're a chauvinist," Asperger says. "I wasn't the one who suggested German food! You should get stew put in front of you every day, so you know how hard life can be."

"I could stand that even less than roast pork, sauerkraut, and dumplings! And I'll make the lentils myself! Do we have vinegar? You can forget the Thuringian blood sausage, fried eggs are fine, better actually." —He's actually gotten me to cook.

For his part, he finds double-yolked eggs somewhere, from happy chickens, he claims.

"I know happy chickens, they don't experiment. There's only ever one yolk, and I prefer the brown ones, it's a matter of color."

"Do you know chicken-throwing?" he asks. "The chicken shies away, you grab its underside, the feathers are silky, velvety, with brittle ribs. They make such lovely noises, uuk ukuk uk!, you lift it and throw it over the fence. It flutters, struggles, before it remembers that it's a bird and can fly, and then it lands on the ground, clucking excitedly, agitated and confused by having remembered what to do.

And you catch hold of it again through the chicken wire, the bird doesn't fly off, doesn't run away, lets itself be lifted awkwardly through the mesh until you can grab it properly and throw it again, and once again it flies and is pleased with itself, but first it has to make the same initial fuss, because it has such a short memory. But something of the frisson of delight remains, of its glorious past as a bird. I like the sounds and the color, and how they come running up trustingly, pecking and not thinking about tomorrow. Or even about the next minute. Really not at all."

"They're pretty, the brown ones."

"Just the brown ones? Have you ever seen a German Empire chicken?"

I have to laugh. "Now even poultry is being slapped with the label 'German,' like 'best quality German butter,' I haven't seen that anywhere else."

"Nonetheless, the German Empire chicken is quite good, only the Welsches are better: colorful, small, exemplary breeders."

"What are you even talking about?"

"I used to live in a shared place in Krefeld," he says.

"Where?"

"In a commune."

"They still exist?"

"Yes. A medieval building, a former fort, actually, made of stone. As a guest, you got a vase next to your bed at night, possibly an antique one. Thick walls. We had chickens. I'd volunteered to take care of them. They followed me around. Then it was decided that we'd have to butcher them if we were serious about it. I said leave me out of it, and someone else gave it a try. After that I preferred to do it myself."

"Why kill them at all?"

"Because they breed and it's a necessary part of animal husbandry, those are the rules."

I look at him.

"When they reach a certain age. I didn't want to leave it to anyone else. You have to lay them on their backs. They become rigid, fall into a stupor, and then you can do it. Before, my predecessor . . . I'd never see a chicken without a head . . ."

"Leave it."

"Anyway, it was better that way."

"I know," I say. "In our house my mother had to kill the carp. She could do it. My father—it was his favorite dish, he talked to them while shaving, fed them bread in the bathtub—somehow he always missed, and every time it was a bloodbath. You had to wrap them in a wet dishtowel so they wouldn't slip, and then hit them with the blunt end...no, mother did it with a mallet, with an iron mallet on the head. Sometimes the portioned pieces jumped off the plate in the pantry, once they even jumped out of the soup, very small pieces. As a child I could stand to look at it, the swim bladder, the innards. We were just supposed to watch out for the gallbladder. Greenish-yellow, a tiny pouch. If it burst, the whole thing was for naught, we had to throw the fish away. And if you didn't notice, Christmas dinner was spoiled."

"Why Christmas dinner?" Asperger asks. "New Year's Eve dinner was spoiled. For Christmas there's roast goose."

"We've been through this," I say. "Don't keep confusing things. Carp for Christmas, goose for New Year's, it's simple."

"So what are we going to do," he asks. "Christmas is in a week."

"Nothing. In a week I'll be gone."

"What?"

The doorbell rings. The downstairs neighbor needs eggs. Asperger gets them out of the refrigerator; I didn't even know there were still some there. I was never asked. She's not asking me, really, she's asking Asperger. A friendly old woman, she looks at me with curiosity, apologizes repeatedly. Asperger used her telephone a few times. I notice that this neighborly familiarity makes me happy, even if it's not aimed at me. He talks to her about the water getting turned off again, about when the outage is planned. And that not long ago the electricity was out too. That's when I was still sleeping. I miss every chance of belonging, every bit of fellowship.

Her cat slips in behind her, it's the red one. It rubs itself against their legs, sniffs at the stove, the legs of the chairs, inspects the kitchen, tail lifted. I stoop down to pet it but it dodges, goes to Asperger.

"Salo, come here!"

"What's the cat's name?" I ask, incredulous.

"Salo, from Salome, but she only reacts to the first two syllables; if you say the whole name she tunes it out."

"So she's not called Salome?"

The cat leaves the apartment, goes down the stairs. "I have to go too," says the woman. "I have two fruit loaves in the oven. The children are coming over the holidays. I still have to bake cookies. I'll bring some up!" she calls from the hallway.

"We won't be here," I say, but Asperger has already closed the door. "Why do you have to spoil her pleasure? And where do you want to go, anyway?"

"I have to get back."

"To where?"

"I'm meeting the others in Metz."

"What are you doing there?"

"They're already rehearsing, I've told you."

"They can do that without you."

We're back in the continuous loop we've been in for days; he stubbornly repeats the same sentences, I stubbornly give the same answers.

"And you, don't you have anything to do?" I ask.

"Unlike you, I went to the doctor," he says. "And he gave me a note. I'm unfit to work for at least another week!"

I look at him.

"I don't know anything about you, really, except that you've taken care of chickens and are from Germany."

"That's not entirely true," he says. "Part of my family comes from Iglau."

"What?"

"You'd probably say Jihlava."

"Indeed I would!"

"I don't like the word 'Sudete,' or 'displaced person,' for that matter."

"How very nice of you!"

He's chopping vegetables and refuses to be distracted. I watch him. "And how do you feel about the Pentecost meetings?" I ask crossly.

He laughs. "I was born in the American zone, if that's what you mean. Specifically, in Frankfurt—Free City, not to be conflated with Hessen; as a Praguer you must understand that. But I don't want to bore you with our *internal affairs*. I count Huguenots, Netherlanders, Czechs, and Germans among my ancestors. In the whole family—and my father had nine siblings—there was only one uncle who once went to a Pentecost meeting of the Czech associations; they showed images from the 'homeland.' He'd gotten a head wound clearing away war rubble, when they were demolishing a wall he came down with it. And it was too dumb even for him."

"Too bad, the 'homeland,' is nice," I say. "So, just saints and head cases in your family. No one knew a thing."

"On the contrary, my grandmother was a staunch National-Socialist Women's Leaguer, and proud of it. She'd made it from housemaid to housemisstress, the neighbors finally greeted her. And my mother too only managed to say the word 'Jew' in a whisper for years after the war, as if it were forbidden. At the same time there were Jews from Amsterdam in our clan, just third degree, of course. What do you want to hear about my family, actually?"

"Nothing, actually."

"We had some of everything—there were enough siblings. One was even a Communist, he was drafted into the police after the war."

"In the GDR?"

"No, in the West of course. In the 'Zone,' as we called it, he would have landed in jail; revisionists got special treatment. My father was first locked up by the Nazis for being a Social Democrat, then—pardon me—by the Czechs for being a German, and after deportation by the Americans for being a suspected Nazi, but only briefly. Then he translated for them. It was the expulsion by the Czechs that hurt him the most. He didn't cope well in Germany, it wasn't his landscape. Even though the Allies had decided on the expulsion together, in some places it looked more like revenge, the Czechs were zealous. Not everywhere, but in the border territories there were riots that had nothing to do with any kind of 'democratic tradition.'"

"My compatriots. Who love to play the victim!" I stare out the window; half a frozen deer is being unloaded from the roof of a car.

"What can I say?" He shrugs.

"I'm going into town tomorrow, to meet people, talk to someone."

"I'll come."

"No, I don't want you to."

"Why, because I'm German?"

"You needn't be so conceited about your Germanness, being Czech is no more pleasant, no simpler or more flattering."

"On the contrary, you didn't have a Hitler."

"What I don't have today is hunger. And someone has to tidy this place up!" I throw clothes off the bed.

He collects them; his wallet had fallen out.

"You wanted to know about me," he hands me a business card, shrunken, soggy, the writing hardly legible. "Dr. Thomas Asperger, Euroopa Muusikateatrite Akadeemia." At first I think the Vltava must have smeared the letters, or doubled them. "Is it Finnish?"

"Estonian." He flips the card over. "European Musical Theater Academy. I have it in Czech as well. We have headquarters in Bayreuth, Tallinn, and Prague. I was supposed to go to Tallinn, actually, but my Estonian isn't up to snuff. Czech was spoken at home sometimes in my family; as a child I could sing Czech Christmas songs, I didn't want to lose that. Besides, my favorite uncle is here."

"The one with the head wound?"

"No, Uncle Otto, the singer. You'll meet him."

"That won't be necessary. And what do you do here?"

"Coordinator, it's called. A kind of factotum, girl Friday, Dr. Golz's office boy."

"I'd like a drink."

"Is it such a shock?"

"It's a shock to me that you work at all. You haven't been in for at least ten days."

"Fourteen. But first of all, it's the Christmas holiday, and second of all, I was sick. And when they heard who I was taking care of . . ."

"What?"

"How do you think I know your schedule so well that I could follow you to Strasbourg. And I don't even like ballet. I like what you do. It's a different kind of *Tanztheater*. You can get me with Tchaikovsky's *Pas de deux*! Of course they know you. The Academy has only recently been founded, our mission is to support projects."

"What did you actually study?" I ask.

"History of music and theater, plus four semesters of Egyptology."

"Wrong field, economics would have been better."

"You're right, we didn't even get to the Middle Kingdom, we stopped somewhere around Pepi I. By the way, in the Kinský Palace there's an exhibition on death cults or something, with Egyptian burial chambers. Do you want to go?"

"Into the burial chambers?"

"There are supposed to be some things on loan from China as well."

"The terracotta warriors?"

"I don't know exactly. Maybe there's just a terracotta horse. I really wanted to study Sinology because of the excavated army but the professor hadn't familiarized himself with the discovery yet. Actually I wanted to learn Mongolian as well."

"Because of Temüjin?"

He looks at me. "Yes, before he became Genghis Khan."

"We once tried to dance the secret history of the Mongols," I say.

"Do you dance what you read, not what you hear?"

"Sometimes. I try to find the music at the same time."

"Don't most people do it the other way around?"

"How other people do it is their problem."

"How long have you been the . . . leader?"

I laugh. "Ten years. 'Leader' is right. We're travelling people."

"I've known you a long time. Since *The Makropulos Affair*. Is your name really Marty?"

"Something like that."

"Leonora. Do people call you Lena or Nora?"

"Both. Lena is more familiar."

"To me you were always Marty. What am I to you?"

I consider.

"What was I in the Vltava?"

"In the Vltava you were a lunatic. Then a nurse, a good one, then a chef, unfortunately also a very good one. And now you're a 'Sudete' on top of it!" I laugh. "Where does the word come from, anyway?"

"No idea, my father called himself a Czechoslovak."

"Then he'll soon be the last one."

"That's how it looks at the moment, yes," he says. "In the six months I've lived here, I don't think I've seen the Slovaks accept a single federal decision. Every official state visitor has to make an extra trip to Bratislava, as if the French president had to go from London to Scotland for a treaty to be valid. It's absurd—three administrations: the Czech, the Slovak, and the federal, each one constantly stepping on the others' toes. The Slovaks want to make their own foreign policy, but when it's a matter of finance, they cry for the federation. The Czechs are the opposite: long-suffering patrons, always the older brother, and then suddenly aggrieved. I'm sorry. A few eggs and tomatoes from a handful of hotheads hit the president's parka in Bratislava and they're offended. Fine, he wasn't wearing a parka, as in Prague—he goes to Slovakia properly dressed, he is the president after all. For him it was exciting more than anything—he's a playwright, don't forget. But they go right to ingratitude, they talk of the schools they've established there, schools taught in Slovak—the Slovaks should have stayed with the Hungarians if all they're going to do is complain, they should just leave already! Of course the Slovaks are sensitive. They feel cheated in everything, and now patronized to boot. It was easier with the Hungarians—a clear enemy—but the Czechs? They'll have to give up their positions."

"Which positions? They already did that ages ago."

"Maybe that's what disturbs the Slovaks the most," he says. "They want to be persuaded. The Czechs are taking the easy way out. Where's the plebiscite?"

"The people are asking themselves that too." I look at all the newspapers that have piled up. Something's hissing in the kitchen.

"What's cooking?"

"Chicken paprikash."

"Again?"

"I've never cooked it before, we've just talked about it."

"You've talked about it," I say.

"And to start, real chicken soup, with giblets."

"Like for women after childbirth."

"Who knows?" he laughs.

I could still throw him out. "I'm not eating today! This cooking has to stop."

He's silent.

"Turn it off, please."

"I slave over a hot stove all day . . ." he goes into the kitchen.

"And please stop it with the jokes!"

"Fine, we can talk seriously," he says. "About the Beneš decrees. And that the Munich Agreement was null and void from the start. That at the end of the year the Slovaks will leave and the Czechs will let them. That the Germans shouldn't all have been deported and that the general expulsion was unjust. But we know that. Are we going out?"

He coughs, his eyes gleam.

"It seems we've switched roles," I say. "Wouldn't it be better for you to lie down?"

"Nonsense!" He hands me my coat. The fabric feels stiff; it's the first time I've left the house. The straw bell on the button, the ornament from the Slovakian woman from Old Town Square, is crushed, the bath in the Vltava didn't do it any favors. I leave it on. We go up Petřín, climb up the observation tower, which is open, surprisingly, and go into the mirror maze. It's a sunny day, there's still snow on the ground, Prague is beautiful. We see each other distorted and swollen, stretched, serpentine, with huge heads and short legs; we laugh, throw snowballs. Asperger's eyes shine, I'm not sure whether from fever or joy. He gives me a long look. Your eyes, he says. They're shining.

I don't want to get used to him.

The abrupt transition from strangeness to familiarity, sickness to health: euphoria. A state of ease and persistent joy.

He collects points, plays for time. He doesn't know that with someone like me, time is the enemy. Always on the side of the sure winner, of death.

I don't like to play it safe, don't like games of dead certainty. And no opportunities. I never seize them. I don't even see them. I turn around.

Wait! He runs after me.


That evening I notice that I can no longer stand this closeness, this intimacy bred of illness. "I'm healthy," I say. "I'd like you to leave."

He's silent. After sitting frozen for a long time, he begins gathering his things; he didn't have anything with him, really. He trips over the leg of a chair, his face wet with tears.

"And don't cough!" I leave the room, but there's only one, so I stay in the unheated kitchen. I want to wash the dishes, but everything is already tidy, or make tea at least, but the pot is full. That's what he gets for his solicitousness!

He opens the door, his face downcast, we're both paralyzed, mute with horror. I touch his hand. We get such a shock from the static electricity that we flinch and then start to laugh, he's already pressing his face into my neck and holding me close, I can hardly breathe, we get tears on each other, laugh, taste the salt on our fever-chapped lips. Above us on the poster the three-hundred-year-old Elina Makropulos/Emilia Marty in my form, with my face, springing in a high arc across time.

You can unpack, I say.

Touching an unfamiliar body. A gamble. He has broad shoulders and a strong ribcage, he clasps me tightly and carefully, long, slim legs. I lay my head on his belly, hear the rumbling of his bowels, the long, tortuous path of the humors, his heart. His bosom is almost bigger than mine, with fine curly hair, I suck his nipple, close my eyes. He's motherly.

*Verklärte Nacht*. Transfigured Night. How many times we spin on our own axes, on each other's, his head between my arms, between my legs, warm, round, heavy, it feels like birth and like death, the line isn't clear. I stare at him. Until now he was a stranger, now we're delving into each other, into every wrinkle, every nook of skin, all openings are entrances, and it hurts to separate, to part. It's only for a short moment, only to breathe. This night is a long sickness, fever, delirium; the worst thing that could happen: to recover. Near morning, exhausted, tensely awake: it's enough to look at each other and the frenzy, the feeling for each other, the intertwining starts all over again. We don't know which body part belongs to whom, there are no parts. That's how we fall asleep.

## AFTERWORD

In Ancient Egyptian mythology, transfiguration is what happens when a royal's soul passes from the realm of the living to the realm of the dead, facilitated by elaborate burial rituals, and leading to its elevation. Death is not conceived as the end of life but its transformation and continuation in a different form. In Libuše Moníková's novel, the concept of transfiguration is used metaphorically: it captures the death and rebirth of the author's homeland, whose existence was threatened by political developments after the end of the Cold War. In the early 1990s, expatriate Moníková, whose novels and essays narrate the complicated history and political situation of Czechoslovakia, was faced with the prospect of witnessing her country split apart into two states, the Czech and Slovak Republics, creating an uncertain future for both, and deeply affecting the author's love for her homeland. The anxiety that this political development triggered for the author and her fellow citizens is palpable in the atmosphere of *Transfigured Night,* but it is counterbalanced by the way in which the novel's protagonist, Leonora Marty (an expatriate like the author), is at the same time experiencing a world alive with the cultural traditions preserved in legends, myths, and stories originating in the city of Prague and other cultural traditions. As the choreographer and prima ballerina of an internationally renowned dance company making a guest appearance in Prague, the figure of Leonora literally becomes the image for the tension between past and present, and between the personal and the political—on an advertising poster for her performances, suspended in mid-air as she leaps over the city of Prague, whose towers are visible in the background, the dancing Leonora transfigures space and time—as the author states at the end of the first chapter. The image of the flying dancer from Prague, aloft yet intimately connected to her city, becomes the metaphor and leitmotif for the novel's central themes of life and death, art and reality, and the search for identity between the present self and the many roles an artist might assume while encountering the historical and fictional characters that constitute the narratives of the world.

Libuše Moníková was born in Prague in 1945, where she also grew up and developed her primary identity as a "Prague writer"—in the footsteps of role models from the tradition of Prague German Literature, most prominent among them Franz Kafka. She studied English and German literature at the city's Charles University and wrote a Ph.D. dissertation comparing Shakespeare's and Bertolt Brecht's versions of their drama about the Roman leader Coriolanus. After getting married to a German citizen and teaching literature at several German universities, she turned to full time writing in 1981. Starting out in her native Czech, she quickly realized that the foreign language of German would provide her with an intellectual and emotional distance more appropriate for the delicate topic she was addressing in her first novel, *An Injury* (1981): the rape of a young woman by a policeman. It is a narrative often read allegorically as the rape of her home country by the Soviet intruders, who occupied Prague in 1968 and established their oppressive regime, which would last until the fall of the Iron Curtain in 1989. Before moving to Germany in 1971, and afterwards during many visits, Moníková witnessed this forced transformation of her homeland, whose political liberalization during the "Prague Spring" of 1968 had ended so brutally and abruptly when Soviet tanks rolled onto Wenceslas Square, the nation's political center and stage for many historical events and public demonstrations. An event that disturbed her even more would occur in January 1969, when Prague student Jan Palach self-immolated right there to protest the Soviet invasion. The whole world reacted to Palach's self-sacrifice and so did Moníková, who was in a movie theatre on Wenceslas Square at the time. She chose to dedicate her first book to Jan Palach, and in spirit all her following books. In two of her essays she discusses the 1968 Soviet invasion and the self-immolation of Palach and of several others who followed him as "living torches." To no avail; the following twenty years, the so-called period of "normalization," were years characterized by censorship, surveillance, and oppression. Several of Moníková's novels take place during this time period. With the advent of the Velvet Revolution in November 1989, the collapse of the Soviet Union, and with former dissident and literary author Václav Havel now president, things were looking up for the Czechoslovak nation. However, political tensions between the Slovaks and the Czechs led to a Slovak Declaration of Independence and the break-up of the country into two states. Along with her fellow writer, moral authority, and now the country's most powerful man, Václav Havel, Moníková opposed the dissolution of her homeland, for which Jan Palach and many before and after had sacrificed so much. *Transfigured Night* takes place in this uneasy political atmosphere towards the end of 1992, in the months leading up to Czechoslovakia's split into two states on January 1, 1993.

In all of her novels, Moníková incorporates historical events and developments that she had personally experienced. She then weaves these political-personal portraits of her time together with the deeper history of her homeland as well as with discussions of the rich cultural tradition that shapes a nation state just as much as political events do. Her second novel, *Pavane for a Deceased Princess* (1983) shares numerous characteristics with *Transfigured Night:* Both narratives are deeply personal, featuring a female first-person narrator who in many ways is an alter ego of the author—though she is also fictionalized. Both narratives borrow their title from of a piece of classical music: in the first case it is French composer Maurice Ravel's *Pavane pour une infante défunte* (1899 for solo piano; 1910 for orchestra); and for *Transfigured Night* it is German composer Arnold Schönberg's string sextet *Verklärte Nacht* (Transfigured Night, also 1899). These book titles already point to what Moníková would develop into her major literary device when composing a fictional text: she interweaves descriptions of images, observations, her vast knowledge, and borrowed techniques from works of art in other media, such as music, fine art, film, and dance. This results in her texts' "intermediality"—an opening up of the linguistic medium to incorporate the traditions and characteristics of other media. This method enriches her literary text and makes it multi-dimensional since it creates an imaginary in the reader's mind that goes beyond language and establishes connections to the cultural world in communication with her literary text. In one of her essays, Moníková explains the source of this approach: authors and artists do not create in a vacuum; they all "stand on the shoulders of giants"—those, who have created works of art before them, for centuries or millennia, especially the most famous authors and artists in every medium. Such giants are both frightening and helpful: will the writer or artist looking up to them ever be as good, as successful, and as highly respected? Literary critic Harold Bloom famously called this a writer's "anxiety of influence"—the fear of being so overwhelmed by the giants' great works that it might become impossible to create one's own independent and original work. But since the giants provide models from which to learn there is also a chance to be even better: after all, whoever stands on their shoulders will benefit and see even farther than they do. As a voracious reader, listener to music, attendee at opera and dance performances, film buff, museum visitor, and—in the case of visual art—a close personal friend of contemporary Czech artists, Moníková had a treasure trove of works of art as material at her intellectual disposal, from which she could draw to incorporate allusions, evocations, and descriptions. At times she would even simulate their techniques in her own medium of the literary language, such as reproducing the film technique of the "hard cut" in the flow of her narrative by creating paragraphs sharply contrasting in topic and atmosphere, or by mimicking slow motion and camera zoom by gradually increasing the details of her description. For music, she primarily chose to represent how a listener would be emotionally affected but twice she also used the title and its meaning to set the tone for her narrative: in the case of *Pavane* this creates a somber and melancholic atmosphere; for *Transfigured Night* it emphasizes the almost magical feelings that the protagonist is allowed to have even as she experiences her homeland's troublesome situation as a kind of personal identity crisis.

The two narratives are actually connected in further ways, although in this case they seem to make up the two sides of one coin: while *Transfigured Night* is all about an expat's experience in her homeland of Czechoslovakia, *Pavane* portrays the life of a woman who lives as a foreigner in Germany and reacts to many forms of discrimination and exclusion, because of both her gender and her status as a foreigner. Both novels also contain a love story, though the one in *Transfigured Night* is more central to the narrative. Also of significance in both texts is the theme of death and how, in each case, the protagonist is fighting against its threats and temptations, with unusual means. In addition, in many ways, *Pavane,* written thirteen years earlier, is a text in which the author is still working out her identity as a Czech national and writer of literature in German—like the famous literary giant from Prague on whose shoulders she is thus standing: Franz Kafka (1883–1924). In addition to the intermedial references to music and film, the narrative is woven through with intertextual passages, in which the author's alter ego is "rectifying" Kafka's texts, wrapping up her own novel with a passage that provides a new ending to Kafka's unfinished novel *The Castle* (1926). In her last rewritten, "rectified" passage, she has one of Kafka's female characters leave the depressed and oppressive situation of the village behind, symbolically cross a bridge, and actively choose her own path, with a Beatles song on her lips that provides the last words of both the narrator's and Moníková's own novel: "she's leaving home, bye, bye." It is a kind of departure for the author; from now on she will confidently write her own texts and will do so from the superior position of someone with the authority to playfully and humorously deal with her literary predecessor. In her next novel, she grants Kafka an appearance in a narrated comic strip sequence.

Moníková's third novel is her own castle-novel and her magnum opus not just in length (440 pages); she received the Döblin-Prize for it. It takes place in 1970s Czechoslovakia, features four male protagonists, and exposes one of the main issues of the time of "normalization" when the country was a part of the Soviet empire: how to survive as an artist in this restrictive atmosphere under censorship, keeping up the outer appearances of one's life as a citizen while at the same time working to undermine and subvert the oppressive system through art; fittingly, this novel is titled *The Façade* (1987; English trans., 1991). Four Czech artists work under a state contract restoring the façade of a large Bohemian Renaissance castle in the town of Litomyšl but at the same time they smuggle in their critical views, change some of the images on the façade in order to rewrite (or "rectify," like the narrator in *Pavane*) the narrative of their country's history, and are also able to mount an exhibition of their own work despite lacking permits for it. This is the way most writers and artists at the time, having to navigate through the choppy waters of prohibitions, bans, and harrassment by state officials, had to operate, within a so-called grey zone that would still provide them some freedom of expression for their own artistic ideas. Moníková based her characters on a team of real-life Czech painters and sculptors: Zdeněk Palcr (1927–1996), Stanislav Podhrázský (1920–1999), Olbram Zoubek (1926–2017), and Václav Boštík (1913–2005). They restored Litomyšl castle beginning in 1974, dedicating every summer to this project for many years. Since she was a close friend of Palcr, Moníková was able to visit the restoration site and take photographs, which later allowed her to write precise descriptions of the images covering the façade and of the restoration. This process, in which layers upon layers of earlier versions of the images are exposed—as in a palimpsest—and are then either restored or replaced, has often been read allegorically as a restoration of Czech and Bohemian history in opposition to (and "rectifying") the official version of history spread by the Soviet oppressors. It is an example of how art and literature can counteract the actions of unethical political forces. The second part of the novel takes the reader along to Siberia, where Palcr gets stuck in a snowstorm en route to a project in Japan, then gets trapped in the Soviet science center Akademgorodok because they fear he may be a spy, but he also has unique experiences with the indigenous population that—like the Czechs—is suffering from and fighting political oppression originating in distant Moscow. While in her first two novels the human body is the site of national and personal trauma, in *The Façade* the trauma of political oppression is projected outward onto the castle façade, which can be manipulated by the artists, who are thus able to properly rewrite the nation's history. Since the focus is on the process of this rewriting, the novel can be classified as historiographic metafiction—a fictional text not just about history, but about how to write history, even under an oppressive regime.

Moníková's humorous and slapstick approach to a difficult situation in *The Façade* is, however, counterbalanced again by her last, unfinished novel *Dizziness* (published postumously in 2000), which also deals with the issue of art under political censorship and was supposed to complement *The Façade* as a second major novel. It takes place in the same time frame and follows the life of one artist, Brandl, who teaches at the art academy in Prague. He is constantly subjected to grueling interrogations, harrassment, and surveillance, all of which destroy his physical and emotional health. While writing it, Moníková was suffering from an aggressive brain tumor that would eventually take her life in January 1998, when she was only 52 years of age. Some of the pain of her illness may have been projected onto her protagonist Brandl, who experiences falls and other symptoms as a result of the abuse he is subjected to by his secret service interrogators. He finds solace by immersing himself in the work of French naïve painter Henri Rousseau (1844–1910), who, like so many artists in Czechoslovakia, was at first misunderstood by his contemporaries—but later recognized as a genius.

In between *The Façade* and her last unfinished novel, and in addition to political and literary essays published first in the press and then in two volumes, Moníková wrote two more novels, which take on the topics of film and dance. Her 1992 novel *Drift Ice* begins in Greenland and follows a Czech school teacher on his trip to an conference for educators, which Moníková heavily satirizes. Most of the narrative then elaborates the complicated love story between him and a young Czech woman, contrasting their different experiences growing up a generation apart in Prague during the Second World War in his case, and the 1960s and 1970s in hers. Yet the two are both movie buffs and connect over sharing this love with each other—after all, he looks like Richard Burton, and she looks like Elizabeth Taylor. Describing her characters' looks in such a way instantly evokes this famous film couple's real-life stormy relationship as well as their many movie roles as a pair— and the reader, who is likely familiar with these big-screen actors and their roles, can easily imagine how this relationship, is going to develop. Intermediality in this novel is all about film—a large number of film titles, directors, actors, and plots are discussed—and the place where it is experienced, the movie theatre. During the time in which Moníková grew up and attended university in Prague, the city had a lively cinema scene with showings of all the major films of the French New Wave, American Westerns and other Hollywood films, Japanese, British, Swedish, German, and other international films, and, of course, Czech and Soviet productions. Moníková would see them all, and both her vast knowledge of film history and her familiarity with the cinema as a place of escape from a challenging reality and even of clandestine subversion of political oppression have shaped her depiction of this medium in her novels. It is the medium she knew best from her own experience. The fact that film has characters, language, and a narrative not unlike those of a novel of course makes its intermedial transfer to the written text easier. And the reverse would also be true: her cinematic way of writing renders her texts the perfect scripts for film productions. One of her main ambitions actually was to have her novels adapted to film, and in 1995 she was contacted by Austrian director Peter Zeitlinger about filming *An Injury*. Their development of the script made good progress but unfortunately funding fell through. Already in 1994, in connection with her honorary position as writer-in-residence in the city of Mainz, funded by one of Germany's major public TV stations, she had been provided a film team that would allow her to produce a documentary film for television. She chose to take them to Greenland, a place that had fascinated her ever since writing *Drift Ice*, and would use the opportunity to create an essay film about the tension between Greenland's beauty and the harsh life of its residents. She also used the opportunity to discuss the fruitful relationship and beneficial exchange between the medium of film and the medium of books.

While *Drift Ice* takes its readers along to Greenland and Austria, Moníková finally, with her fifth fictional narrative, writes a "Prague novel," *Transfigured Night* (1996). It was likely prompted by the political developments after the fall of the Iron Curtain in 1989 and the complications leading up to the country's split into two nations in 1993, when a time of great hope had quickly turned into new upheaval, unease, and uncertainty. For her, this may have triggered the wish for reaffirmation of what Czechoslovak or Czech identity actually is, and what it might mean to her. Since a national definition had been called into doubt once more, and knowing that her country was not solely defined by its political trajectory over centuries of oppression, she turned to its cultural identity that had always persevered and also connected her nation internationally: art knows no borders, and artists create and find a way to share their work both locally and with a wider European and world audience, even when an Iron Curtain tries to block that. One of Moníková's goals was to bring her country's rich cultural traditions again to the attention of her Western audience and highlight the connections that had flourished and survived through multiple occupations by the surrounding imperialist forces, such as the Austro-Hungarian Empire, National Socialist Germany, and the Soviet Union. She wanted to reintegrate Czech culture into European culture, to which it had always belonged, though Western perception of this had been affected by the European East/West split and reduced connections during the Cold War in the second half of the twentieth century. Ultimately, she wanted to bring Czechs and Germans, or more broadly Eastern and Western Europeans, together again, now that this seemed possible, though by no means easy, given their problematic history. These are some of the overarching themes of *Transfigured Night*, and in order to show and reestablish a closer relationship between her two countries, Moníková portrays a developing love story that is based on a shared cultural history that spans all different media—music, dance, film, and art—and interweaves fiction and reality to create a vision of a better common future.

*Transfigured Night* is the story of Leonora Marty, a Czech choreographer, principal, and director of her own dance company, which she founded ten years ago while living abroad. Like Moníková herself, Leonora had left her homeland in 1971 and then taught literature at several German universities—and as in *Pavane*, this first-person narrator is an alter ego of the author but clearly also contains fictional elements and enacts the roles of famous figures whom the author herself admired. When starting her dance company, Leonora specializes in her own form of intermediality, in the opposite direction than Moníková: she adapts literature to her medium—she choreographs and dances literature. In her star role, and because dance requires music, this actually involves three media: Czech writer Karel Čapek's drama *The Makropulous Affair* (1925, sometimes translated as *The Makropulos Case*) was adapted in 1926 to an opera of the same name by Czech composer Leoš Janáček. To top things off, Leonora Marty shares her last name with the protagonist of this drama and opera: Emilia Marty. However, this figure has changed identities and names multiple times and impersonated a whole series of individuals over the course of her long life of 337 years. Her immortality stems from a potion given to her to test its safety by her father, physician and alchemist at the court of Bohemian King Rudolf II. Leonora is really just another reincarnation of the legendary figure of the court physician's immortal daughter. In fact, the motif of impersonation and reincarnation, which also further spins out the idea of standing on the shoulders of giants, recurs repeatedly throughout the narrative. When Leonora falls ill with a fever and hallucinates, she imagines herself in several roles: first, Elina Makropulos as a young daughter; then as the female Egyptian pharaoh Hatshepsut during the process of mummification, which would lead to her transfiguration; and finally as the famous 20th century German film director Leni Riefenstahl—though this last identification turns out to be highly problematic since Riefenstahl was Hitler's filmmaker and lacked an ethical approach to filmmaking.

In a world dominated by great men, Leonora is clearly seeking out female role models and great women with whom to identify. In the same vein, Moníková is changing the gender for her choreographer/dancer protagonist from the original model she used for this figure. Leonora is female even though her life, philosophy of dance and choreography, and many other details, are modeled after a famous real-life male choreographer: fellow Czech expatriate and star choreographer Jíři Kylián (born 1947, in Prague). Just like Moníková and Leonora, Kylián left Czechoslovakia in order to find better professional opportunities in Western Europe (he left in 1967). After dancing in England and with the renowned

Nederlands Dans Theater (NDT), he joined the Stuttgart Ballet in Germany, under its world-famous director, John Cranko. Cranko's sudden death on a transatlantic flight, and Kylián's grief about this tremendous loss, made him choreograph a tribute piece entitled *Return to a Foreign Land* (1974)—it is his first dance set to the music of a Czech composer, Leoš Janáček, and many others would follow. The title of this piece captures the feelings evoked by a loss of the familiar, whether it is the sudden death of one's friend and mentor, or—a feeling well known to both Moníková and Kylián—the kind of estrangement felt by expatriates upon returning to their homeland after a long time away and experiencing it as changed, as foreign. At one point Leonora even asks herself "Is this still my Prague"? Kylián returned to Czechoslovakia several times, in 1982, 1991, and 1995, each time as an internationally renowned dancer and choreographer (in 1977 he had become the director of the famous NDT), similar to Leonora, who also acquired her fame abroad. Film director Hans Hulscher made a documentary about Kylián and his return to Prague, which was broadcast several times on Czech TV in the early nineties. It contains many details that Moníková incorporates into her story about Leonora: she, too, choreographs her ballets using Janáček's music; a party in the Rainbow Room in Rockefeller Center in New York City that Kylián describes in the film gets "translated" into Leonora's party in a Prague hotel—also with a spectacular view; Kylián founded a special group for aging dancers, talks extensively about his grandmother, and has dedicated his ballet *Sinfonietta* to her; Leonora wants to choreograph a ballet called *The Grandmother* (also an allusion to a famous Czech novel of the same title, by literary giant Božena Němcová)—these are just a few examples of the parallels in their lives. In addition, Leonora's style of choreography is modeled after Kylián's, and the signature leaps of his dancers high above the stage become Moníková's central image and metaphor for Leonora and her art that tries to connect the reality of her expatriate existence as an international star with her conflicting feelings of belonging to and simultaneously feeling estranged from the city of Prague and the Czechoslovak nation that is about to be dismantled. As the narrator states at the end of the novel, "she leaps in a high arch over time"—other than the leap through space on a stage, this is a leap that is possible only in the realm of literature. It is a metaphor for Leonora's attempt to reconcile time and space, her return to her homeland with all her personal memories that get evoked as well as the nation's history and uncertain future, and her art, which conquers space through controlled bodily movements but also contains the element of time. As a performance, dance is ephemeral, but recordings and photographs of the dancer flying through the air preserve the artistic achievement, symbolism, and beauty.

However, the narrative takes place after Leonora's company has already left Prague; she has stayed behind in order to reconnect with her city on a more personal level, to "have it all to herself." Her walks, museum visits, attendance at performances, and meeting with a former fellow student all trigger memories of her childhood and youth under the Communist regime that suppressed the development of individuality in favor of producing socialist citizens that would just be a part of the whole. An example of this is her childhood memory of the Spartakiad, the sports competition of the Eastern Bloc similar to the Olympic Games, where she had to dance as one of the many color dots that would form the living images during the ceremony in Strahov stadium. Moníková's description of these socialist games is partly comical, partly satirical, but also shows how her fellow citizens enjoyed them and included their own Bohemian folk traditions. However, she criticizes the nostaglia that was evoked when documentaries of the games were shown on TV in the nineties, ignoring the suffering under Soviet oppression that had otherwise dominated people's lives.

Ironically, it is a descendant of Sudeten Germans who helps Leonora come to terms with her country's complicated history. The Sudeten Germans were ethnic Germans who had started to live in the border regions of the Kingdom of Bohemia many centuries ago. In 1938, with the Munich Agreement, Hitler annexed the territory. Since most of the roughly three million Sudeten Germans were supportive of the National Socialists, they were violently expelled from their land after the end of WWII. To this very day, the issue of the Sudeten Germans is a controversy that affects Czech-German relations on both personal and political levels. The theatregoer who befriends and romantically pursues Leonora after what seems like a chance encounter at the opera but was actually planned by him, Dr. Thomas Asperger, works for the European Music Theatre Academy that maintains an office in Prague. It is his job to find projects to support and he has scoped out Leonora's performances across Europe. For many reasons, Leonora resists his advances but his charm, wit, and intimate familiarity with the history of music, theatre, and dance, including Czech artists, as well as his command of the Czech language, do impress her. When they walk through Prague together and fall into the river Vltava, causing her to become ill, he ends up taking care of her. Only toward the end of the novel does she finally express an interest in him, finding out about his Sudeten German ethnicity. But he immediately qualifies it by explaining that Hugenots, Dutchmen, Czechs, and Germans were among his ancestors—defying any of her attempts to categorize and treat him with prejudice (which she had tended to do earlier). Unlike Romeo and Juliet and many other real and literary star-crossed couples, and after overcoming the difficulties resulting from their countries' complicated history and lingering present issues, Leonora finally gives in to a more intimate connection—a glimmer of hope for the future.

*Transfigured Night* is a complex narrative presenting a dense web of intertextual and intermedial references and allusions, anchoring it firmly in the international history of Western and Eastern European art and literature. Since Moníková's Western readers may not be so familiar with the political and cultural history of Prague and the Czech Republic, she includes many observations of events, localities, and people—instead of describing the well-known tourist spots. She makes sure to discuss the painful shared history as well: the dialogues between Thomas and Leonora can also be read allegorically as leading to a better understanding between their countries.

All of Moníková's novels are in essence political novels that illuminate the history of her beloved country within the European context, rectifying the official history of its oppressors, and aiming to refamiliarize her Western audience with their neighbor that had been hidden behind the Iron Curtain for so long. While political history is full of injuries and painful events and developments, the shared cultural history of Central and Western Europe can provide many points of connection, be it Mozart finishing the composition of his opera *Don Giovanni* in Prague, Janáček's operas and Kylián's ballets contributing to the international music and dance scene, French New Wave Cinema's international success, or painter Henri Rousseau's late fame celebrated in Prague and across the world. Moníková's thinking and writing happened through analogy—perceiving similarities and connections across media, and between different artists and their works of art. Similarities in appearance, sound, shape, or any other characteristic triggered her associations that would then become allusions and direct references in her work, thus linguistically simulating a postmodern collage that conveys the impression of a multilayered "hypertext," as digital media theorist Wolfgang Coy has observed. The breadth and depth of meaning present in a literary text is what characterizes the work of the literary predecessors Moníková admired and drew inspiration from, such as Kafka, Joyce, Pynchon, Dostoevsky, and Arno Schmidt. Except for her literary entanglements with Kafka, these connections remain largely unexplored in the community of literary scholars. Despite her position on the shoulders of literary and artistic giants, Moníková's perception of the world around her, and her way of narrating her observations and aesthetic experiences, is original and unique in German literature and in world literature, and this has been officially recognized. During her barely two decades of writing and publishing her work, she received twelve literary and other awards, among them the Franz Kafka Prize (1989), the Adalbert von Chamisso Prize given for German literature by non-native authors (1991), the Berlin Literature Prize (1992), and the Arno Schmidt Prize (on the day of her passing, January 12, 1998). In 1996, the Federal Republic of Germany honored her with the Cross of Merit for her literary achievement as well as her outstanding efforts towards improving German-Czech relations. And in 1997, the president of the Czech Republic awarded her one of the country's highest honors, the Masaryk Medal. Translations of her work into—so far—ten European languages continue to spread this transnational author's message and efforts to foster mutual understanding, respect, and love among the nations of Europe and the world.

Helga G. Braunbeck<br>
North Carolina State University

Writers slip through the cracks and fail to make a lasting impact in their home countries, not to mention abroad, all the time—in fact, this is more the exception than the rule. Usually, there's a reason, whether a good one or a bad one: the work is "difficult," it is too specific to attract a large audience, it's simply long or simply not that good. As a translator—a chronic champion of lost causes and one whose task, among other things, is to catch gems that have fallen through the cracks—I have such a pile of these gems stored up that I sometimes think there can be no more to find: that anything else brought to my attention is likely to be unknown to me for good reason. Libuše Moníková's *Transfigured Night* is a stunning exception. That Moníková is, despite being published by one of Germany's premier publishing houses and winning numerous prizes, at best a cult favorite there and little known abroad seems to me to be much more an accident of history—her own and Europe's—than a comment on her artistic power and resonance. Indeed, reading Moníková for the first time I was reminded of several Eastern European writers who have become, if not household names, at least cherished members of the growing canon of contemporary international literature in English: Dubravka Ugrešić and Olga Tokarczuk, both of whom share Moníková's feminism, concern with the personal effects of history, and marriage of the encyclopedic and the personal. I was reminded just as much, however, of Renata Adler: an American author (as much as Moníková is a German author, which is to say, by choice rather than by birth) once cult now canon, similarly compendious, with narrators who are likewise irresistible in their prickliness.

My sympathy for the book began as early as the title (*Verklärte Nacht* in the original), which is simultaneously the title of a piece of music—a string sextet by Arnold Schönberg. This very much sets the tone for Moníková's project. As Helga Braunbeck mentions in her afterword, Moníková is known for her profuse reference to other pieces and forms of art. And indeed "reference" downplays the technique by suggesting something ancillary: in fact, just as the title is built on allusion, so is the rest of the book—hardly a page goes by without mention of an artwork, building, legend, or other concrete historical or cultural phenomenon. The pace is breathtaking: Hatshepsut one paragraph, Leni Riefenstahl the next. Yet the approach is neither ekphrastic nor didactic, which makes these references, to my mind, all the more successful. Instead of attempting to evoke other media—whose power by nature lies in their very otherness—Moníková for the most part simply mentions and incorporates—pointing, summarizing, or quoting rather than describing or evoking. Despite the narrator's literary background and repeated comment on her own "addiction" to words, it is striking that in a list of those that "catch" her ("conversion, dislocation, harmonogram, ravaged") there are no adjectives or adverbs. It is the nouns that have power, the name of the thing rather than its depiction. Thus the book reaches outside itself in a way an ekphrastic work does not: it is hard to avoid the temptation, as a reader, to be constantly Googling and Youtubing, looking to experience firsthand just what snatches of tunes and glimpses of images are floating around in the narrator's head.

I speak of the reader, of which a translator is a special kind, but a kind nonetheless. For me the "research" involved in translating this book—which I put in quotes to skirt the suggestion that it was for the most part tedious, and involved either dusty libraries or statistics—was not a temptation but sometimes a necessity, and always a great pleasure. In this case, my research took me to the Berliner Staatsoper to hear Leoš Janáček's *Makropulos Affair* and to the Opéra National de Lyon to see Jiří Kylián's *Gods and Dogs*, and led me to spend a day giggling and sending friends pictures I'd found of posed taxidermied frogs in Estavayer-le-Lac—among many, many other things. These are not activities on which the work depends, far from it. Rather, they were experiences I sought out because Moníková's book made me crave them as part of a desire to be with, get to know, follow the narrator.

The images and music and coordinates the narrator mentions are in fact what make her who she is and what tell her story. It is impossible to speculate on the experience of reading this book before the internet: I can only say that assuming the split-second access it affords us, Moníková's collage technique allows incredible intimacy between reader and narrator. On one level, the book is a portrait of a city, a snapshot of a very specific place at a very specific time. But as the very first sentence performs, it is not a guidebook for outsiders but a trail of breadcrumbs around a city whose implicit audience, it seems to me, both knows it and can benefit from Moníková's commentary: an audience, perhaps, very like the narrator (and author) herself, an exiled Praguer returning after a long absence. Yet the real audience, and the translator, are not necessarily among the cognoscenti. Thus the text cannot feel like it is teaching us: we're invited to simply follow along, jumping from the 22 tram to memories of shared Socialist rituals to the public swimming pool—which particular swimming pool is obvious, it feels. And in fact it is: Moníková's brilliant trick is to lay her breadcrumbs with such clarity and confidence that we feel sure of the path whether we take a glance at the map (or encyclopedia, or internet) or not. In other words: she is generous enough both to assume her reader's knowledge and to lead her agreeably to discover what she does not know without excluding her. In this way, the book is relentlessly inviting: both in the sense of welcoming and in the sense of asking one to come toward it.

Ironically, this warmth and intimacy is packaged as its very opposite: in the first chapter, the narrator is at her most performatively callous, daring us to judge her, to be put off enough to stop reading. As with her eventual lover, Asperger, however, all attempts to push us away have the opposite effect, and our fascination with Leonora Marty is rewarded. The longer we stick around, bearing the tone that is brusque without being sarcastic, melancholy yet charismatic, the more personal the narrative becomes, the more feeling the narrator shows, until ultimately the book ends in a flurry of passion which is all the more rewarding for being delayed and sudden.

*Transfigured Night* is not a long book, and it is often sad when a wonderful book comes to an end, particularly if one is its translator. In its intensity and generosity, however, it does not feel short, and I did not feel sad to finish it. It opens windows to so many other places and works that "finishing" the translation was no end at all—I am still surrounded by the cultural and emotional riches that have come into my life because of it. In short, it is a gem, and I feel lucky to have had the opportunity to translate it.

Anne Posten
Berlin, November 2022

## ABOUT THE TRANSLATOR

**Anne Posten** is a literary translator based in Berlin. She holds an MFA in Creative Writing and Literary Translation from Queens College, CUNY, and a Bachelor's in German from Oberlin College. Her translation of Anja Kampmann's *High as the Waters Rise* was a finalist for the 2020 National Book Award.

**Published titles**

Zdeněk Jirotka: *Saturnin* (2003, 2005, 2009, 2013; pb 2016)
Vladislav Vančura: *Summer of Caprice* (2006; pb 2016)
Karel Poláček: *We Were a Handful* (2007; pb 2016)
Bohumil Hrabal: *Pirouettes on a Postage Stamp* (2008)
Karel Michal: *Everyday Spooks* (2008)
Eduard Bass: *The Chattertooth Eleven* (2009)
Jaroslav Hašek: *Behind the Lines: Bugulma and Other Stories* (2012; pb 2016)
Bohumil Hrabal: *Rambling On* (2014; pb 2016)
Ladislav Fuks: *Of Mice and Mooshaber* (2014)
Josef Jedlička: *Midway upon the Journey of Our Life* (2016)
Jaroslav Durych: *God's Rainbow* (2016)
Ladislav Fuks: *The Cremator* (2016)
Bohuslav Reynek: *The Well at Morning* (2017)
Viktor Dyk: *The Pied Piper* (2017)
Jiří R. Pick: *Society for the Prevention of Cruelty to Animals* (2018)
*Views from the Inside: Czech Underground Literature and Culture (1948–1989)*, ed. M. Machovec (2018)
Ladislav Grosman: *The Shop on Main Street* (2019)
Bohumil Hrabal: *Why I Write? The Early Prose from 1945 to 1952* (2019)
*Jiří Pelán: *Bohumil Hrabal: A Full-length Portrait* (2019)
*Martin Machovec: *Writing Underground* (2019)
Ludvík Vaculík: *A Czech Dreambook* (2019)
Jaroslav Kvapil: *Rusalka* (2020)
Jiří Weil: *Lamentation for 77,297 Victims* (2021)
Vladislav Vančura: *Ploughshares into Swords* (2021)
Siegfried Kapper: *Tales from the Prague Ghetto* (2022)
Jan Zábrana: *The Lesser Histories* (2022)
Jan Procházka: *Ear* (2022)
*A World Apart and Other Stories: Czech Women Writers at the Fin de Siècle* (2022)

**Forthcoming**

Ivan M. Jirous: *End of the World – Poetry and Prose*
Jan Čep: *Common Rue*
Jiří Weil: *Moscow – Border*

*Scholarship

MODERN SLOVAK CLASSICS

**Published titles**
Ján Johanides: *But Crime Does Punish* (2022)

**Forthcoming**
Ján Rozner: *Seven Days to the Funeral*